My Unscripted Life

ALSO BY LAUREN MORRILL

Meant to Be

Being Sloane Jacobs

The Trouble with Destiny

My Unscripted Life

LAUREN MORRILL

Delacorte Press

 Published in the United States by Delacorte Press, an imprint of Random House Children's Books, a division of Penguin Random House LLC, New York.

Delacorte Press is a registered trademark and the colophon is a trademark of Penguin Random House LLC.

randomhouseteens.com

Educators and librarians, for a variety of teaching tools, visit us at RHTeachersLibrarians.com

Library of Congress Cataloging-in-Publication Data
Names: Morrill, Lauren, author.
Title: My unscripted life / Lauren Morrill.
Description: First edition. | New York : Delacorte Press, [2016]
Summary: Working as a summer intern on the set of a movie being filmed in her small Georgia town, seventeen-year-old Dee meets famous pop star turned actor Milo Ritter, who is offending everyone with his rudeness.
Identifiers: LCCN 2015029977 | ISBN 978-0-553-49801-1 (hc) | ISBN 978-0-553-49802-8 (glb) | ISBN 978-0-553-49803-5 (ebook)
Subjects: | CYAC: Motion pictures—Production and direction—Fiction. | Internship programs—Fiction. | Love—Fiction.
Classification: LCC PZ7.M82718 My 2016 | DDC [Fic]—dc23

The text of this book is set in 12-point Electra LH.

Printed in the United States of America
10 9 8 7 6 5 4 3 2 1
First Edition

For Freddie, while you were sleeping

My Unscripted Life

FADE IN:

EXT. QUAINT DOWNTOWN

The sun is high and hot in the cloudless sky. The air is thick, and the pavement seems to sizzle.

PAN DOWN TO:

EXT. COFFEE SHOP—DAY

DEE WILKIE is sitting at a table with her best friend, NAZANEEN PARAD, and she is sweating.

A lot.

One

"And thus begins the worst summer of my life." I lean back, kick off my flip-flops underneath the table, and cross my ankles in the empty chair across from me. My thick curls are stuck to the back of my neck. It's only the first day of summer break, still May, but it's already impossibly steamy outside. A south Georgia summer feels sort of like living in an old man's armpit for three months (four in a bad year).

"Don't be overdramatic," Nazaneen says, never taking her eyes off the baseball game streaming on her phone. The game is the reason we're sitting outside on a day like today. Service is spotty from inside the old brick-and-plaster walls of the Coffee Cup, Wilder's one and only coffeehouse (unless you count the Starbucks inside the Target, which I don't).

Parking at a table at (or in front of, depending on the Mets' schedule) the Coffee Cup has been part of our summer routine since freshman year, when our parents finally started letting us bike downtown by ourselves. I would sketch while Naz watched Mets games or read recaps or compiled stats, and we'd munch stale pastries and suck down oversugared coffee drinks. But today my sketchbook is lying unopened on the table, a pencil tucked into the elastic band holding the covers shut. I'm carrying it around now mostly out of habit. I haven't felt much like drawing lately, not since I got my rejection letter. But I don't really know what to do with myself without a pencil in my hand. My fingers feel twitchy, and I can't stop fidgeting in my chair. I sketch like some people bite their nails or crack their knuckles. It's a physical impulse, and though I feel miles away from any real desire to do it, my body hasn't quite caught up.

When Nazaneen's game goes to commercial, she curses the Mets for being down four runs, then glances up at me. "Your summer is going to be fine," she says. She reaches for her iced double-shot mocha and takes a long sip.

"How is that humanly possible? I have no plans and no best friend, *and* I'm faced with the prospect of no future," I say. I grimace at the whine that's creeping into my voice, but I can't help it. I wad up my straw wrapper and flick it at her, then give her the most sarcastic double-thumbs-up I can muster. "Yay! Hooray! Best summer *ever*!"

Nazaneen rolls her eyes. "You should have applied to the drama department."

"No, I shouldn't have applied at all and saved myself the rejection," I say. In one week, Naz is leaving for Savannah to spend her summer in the Georgia Governor's Honors School program for STEM. And in one week, I will *not* be going with her to the Governor's Honors Fine Arts program. Hence, no best friend and no summer plans. I let myself imagine what my summer would be like if I hadn't been rejected. If I were still living in ignorant bliss that I could cut it as an artist instead of sitting here feeling like a big fish stuck swimming in my teeny, tiny pond. But that future has been so thoroughly obliterated that I can barely conjure it anymore. All I see is eight weeks of sitting at this table, alone, sweating and sucking down iced caffeine so I don't die from boredom or heat stroke.

There's also the chance that I'll be spending the summer filing transcripts at the Wilder College admissions office, a job my dad assures me won't be completely mind-numbing, or feeling my butt calcify in an SAT prep class (that one was all my mother). My parents acted like these were suitable alternatives to GHP. I couldn't tell if they seriously believed it or were just putting on happy faces for me. Either way, neither one is how I want to spend my summer.

"What you need is a distraction," Naz says.

"Truer words . . . ," I reply, but before she can offer up any suggestions, someone on her screen does something big and great, and she's fist-pumping and bouncing in her chair. I've lost her until the next commercial break.

A car pulls up to the stoplight in front of the cafe and screeches to a halt. It's a shiny black compact sports car, and right away I know the driver isn't from around here. First of all, it's about eleventy bajillion degrees outside, and the top of the convertible is up. (Unless it's raining, this is a top-down kind of town.) And when the driver whips into a parallel spot directly in front of our sidewalk table, I know it for sure. Wilder residents have many skills, but parallel parking is not one of them, which is why there are always so many empty spots along Poplar Street downtown.

The door opens and an older man steps out, his silver hair mussed, partly due to some intricate styling and partly due to the Yankees cap he keeps adjusting on and off his head as he glances up and down the street. His crisp, dark jeans, boat shoes, and white oxford tell me he's not only not from around here, he's from *way* out of town. I can see the shadow of his passenger through the dark tinted windows.

His frantic gaze settles upon Nazaneen and me, though Naz is oblivious. At this point it would take a real live New York Met walking up to our table and sitting down to get her attention.

"Excuse me," the guy says, crossing the sidewalk to our table, "do you know where Roff Avenue is?" He holds up his phone. "My GPS keeps trying to get me to turn onto the train tracks."

I immediately wonder why a handsome, well-dressed guy in an Audi is asking for directions to the part of downtown Wilder where one would stash a body, if there were ever any actual murders in our tiny town.

"Yes, sir, actually your GPS isn't wrong. Roff is immediately after the train tracks." I curve my hand sharply to the left to show him the turn. "It doesn't even look like a road, but it's there."

He stares at me, his eyebrows knit together to form a little canyon of skepticism on his forehead.

"Just trust me and turn," I assure him.

He looks down at his phone screen. "Thanks. You live around here?" Something about his clipped tone makes me think he's not looking for any long answers, so I just nod.

"Well, listen, we're going to be setting up production on a film here." He reaches into his pocket and pulls out a black leather case, smaller than a wallet, and from it he produces a crisp white card and passes it to me. ROBERT LEWIN, it reads in shiny black letters, and underneath in italics, *Producer, Director.* I run my thumb over the raised letters and feel a rush of excitement through my core. This was not at all what I expected when he stepped out of the car. Lawyer? Sure. Doctor? Possibly. But a movie filming in Wilder? *This* is news that qualifies as a distraction. "We're still looking to fill a couple PA spots. Just runner-type stuff, but still. If you're looking for a summer internship, call my office. We can always use a few locals on set."

It's not as big a deal as an actual New York Met, but it's enough to draw Naz's attention from her phone screen and her floundering team. We've just heard that a movie is going to be filming in our small, so-sleepy-as-to-be-in-a-coma hometown.

Naz reaches for the card in my hand and flips it over, as if maybe she's going to find the words "Just kidding!" printed on the other side.

"A movie? For real?" she asks.

"For real," he replies. He sticks out his hand for me to shake. "Rob Lewin." There's a look on his face like maybe we might recognize the name, maybe even that we *should,* but I don't. One glance over at Naz, who is giving him a purposely blank stare, tells me she doesn't either. It's not like we're country bumpkins. We see plenty of movies. Once football season ends, it's pretty much the only thing to do on a Friday night. And I could name most of the actors in them. I've just never really paid much attention to directors other than, you know, Steven Spielberg or Martin Scorsese (he's a director, right?).

"Like, a real movie?" I ask.

"I don't make fake ones," he says.

Naz is still not convinced. "Who's in this *movie*?" She manages to keep her hands from making the implied air quotes, but her voice betrays her heavy skepticism.

"Well, it stars Milo Ritter, and—" Rob begins.

"Oh my God," I blurt out. My voice comes out as a whisper, which is good, because I worried it would be a shout.

"The *singer*?" Naz snorts. I know she's thinking back to our slumber parties the summer between sixth and seventh grades, when we'd make up dances to Milo Ritter songs and perform them for her older sisters in their backyard. We both used to have a poster of him hugging a beagle puppy, his bright blue eyes and white smile beaming down at us from above our respective beds. He was only fifteen when he released his first album, so it was way too easy to crush on him.

Rob chuckles at the mix of shock and disdain. He glances over his shoulder, then back at us, his mouth quirked into a wry smile. "Yeah, the singer. He's trying something new. This'll be his first film."

Naz chuckles too. She hands Rob's card to me, apparently satisfied with his legitimacy. "Good thing," she says. "His last album sucked out loud."

"Naz!" I stare wide-eyed at her.

"What? It was like music to have a coma to," she says, and shrugs.

I shoot Rob an apologetic smile and hold up his business card. "Thanks. I'll have to check with my—" I stop myself just before I say "parents." I barely look my seventeen-almost-eighteen years, so he has to know I'm in high school, but I don't want to seem like a *child.* "I'll think about it and get back to you."

Rob nods. "You talk to your mom and dad and let me know," he says. "Oh, and where's a good place to eat around here?"

"The Diner," Naz and I reply in unison.

"Best burgers in town," I tell him, and point him down the road and around the corner and give him strict instructions to order the fries, extra crispy. He climbs back into the sports car and pulls away.

I watch the taillights disappear around the corner. "Okay,

did that just happen, or am I having a stress-induced stroke?" I feel light and tingly, like I'm in that hazy space between dreaming and awake. Naz, on the other hand, looks completely nonplussed.

"You're definitely having a stroke if you're thinking of calling that guy," she replies.

"What? Why? It's not like I have anything *else* to do this summer."

Naz winces at the reminder of our impending separation. Even though I told her over and over not to, I know she feels guilty for leaving me. It's not her fault the admissions committee immediately recognized her science genius but found my art two rungs below amateur.

"I'm pretty sure doing nothing is better than getting ax-murdered by some 'director,'" she says. This time she definitely hooks her fingers into air quotes.

"You just don't like him because he's a Yankees fan." I wave the business card in her face. "He's legit!"

She snatches it from my grasp. "Lemme see about this." She holds the card in one hand and her phone in the other, typing the name in with her thumb. Within seconds, the screen is filled with links topped by a row of photos of the man who was just standing in front of us.

"Oh my God, is that—" I point, and Naz taps the tiny photo until it fills the screen with Rob in a sharp black tuxedo clutching a shiny golden statue.

"Okay, so he might be legit," Naz says. She clicks back

and opens his ScreenData page. The list of credits for movies and TV shows looks endless—stuff he's written, directed, produced. Some of the titles I recognize, but there's not much listed that I've actually seen. Mostly stuff that gets talked about on the public radio station my parents listen to, mentioned in the same breath as all the major movie awards and festivals. Like I said, I like movies, but I'm not much of a film buff. But just from looking, it's clear he's *definitely* legit.

I take the business card back from Naz and stare at the text. I may not have a best friend, and my future may still be in question, but I may have just solved the summer-plans problem.

INT. DEE'S KITCHEN

DEE is sitting at the kitchen table
with her MOM and DAD.

The business card sits on the table
in front of them.

DEE

Please?

MOM

Are you sure you wouldn't rather take
the admissions office job?

DEE

I'm going to pretend you didn't say
that.

Two

Convincing my parents wasn't nearly as difficult as I'd imagined. One look at Rob's ScreenData page and they agreed to let me work on set. I suspect that I'd done enough moping since my Governor's School rejection had arrived that they would have agreed to just about anything short of a pony to get me to perk up. And they'd only say no to a pony because it would trample my mother's newly seeded lawn. Besides, working on a movie? With Milo Ritter? Yeah, that's *way* better than a pony.

My dad did insist on getting on the phone with Rob (though I think he only managed to get through to his secretary) when I called about the job, and I also had to let him drive me to the studio on my first day (though my bike is in the rack on the back of the car to take me home). I tried to negotiate my way out of it, but it was no use. I think it was equal parts overprotective father and indie film fanboy that played into *that* decision.

"Turn here," I say as we approach Roff Avenue.

"Are you sure?" The blinker clicks, quick, in time with my rapid heartbeat.

I'm sure. They're the directions I gave Rob just a few days ago. We turn on Roff Avenue and bounce down the broken old road, past abandoned warehouses and overgrown factories. At the end of the road, an old office park emerges from the weeds. One of the buildings houses our local UPS depot, surrounded by brown trucks and eighteen-wheelers. Across the way is a drab warehouse with a red sign out front telling me it's the home of Chiron, though I can't even begin to guess what they do in there. The blue swishy logo gives no indication. There's one more building on the lot, and though it has no sign, it must be my destination. I clutch the printout of the email from Rialto Productions. It has directions to production headquarters, along with a call time and some other information.

"I didn't even know this was back here," Dad says as he turns the car into the parking lot. I don't say anything, because all my thoughts—*this looks like the scene of a murder, this looks like where you stash a body, this looks like where you walk into a warehouse and get sucked into a third dimension*—would not instill confidence. And I want him to actually *leave* me here, preferably without coming in first. I know next to nothing about moviemaking, but I'm pretty sure arriving on set with your dad as a chaperone is *not* done.

We pull up to a temporary guardhouse at the entrance, clearly new as part of the production, and stop. A short, squat woman steps out, her hair in braids beneath a black ball cap. "Can I help you?"

My dad leans across my lap to duck through the passenger window, leaving me flattened against the back of the seat. "Yeah, hi, we're here for the movie?" I roll my eyes, but my cheeks burn. Already we sound like celebrity-stalking fans, so I'm not surprised when she narrows her eyes and reaches for a clipboard.

"Name?"

I give Dad a firm but gentle shove and then take my place in the window. "Dee Wilkie," I say.

Her finger scans over the list, pausing to tap on a name. She grabs a neon-green piece of paper off a stack and hands it to me. "Put this in your windshield and park where the yellow sign says CREW." She points down the way toward a sea of cars.

I start to hand the paper back to her. "Oh, he's not—" I say, but Dad plucks the parking pass out of my hand.

"Thank you!" he calls through the open window. He quickly finds an empty space, a cherry-red Mini Cooper on one side and a rusted-out Toyota sedan on the other.

"Dad, you promised," I say as I watch him unbuckle his seat belt. I swallow the whine that wants to creep into my voice. The only way to win this battle is to give the impression that I'm a mature young woman headed to her first day at work, as if I took the filing job at the college that he offered. And maybe if I can conjure up that tone of voice, I'll actually feel like that's what I'm doing. But I'm seriously faking it, because right now I'm so overcome with butterflies and lightning bolts and basically a whole summer-evening storm inside me that I can barely sit still. I settle for giving him a pleading look.

He sighs. I can tell he desperately wants to come in and look around, though not for the benefit of my safety.

"Please, Dad?"

He sighs again. "Don't tell your mother," he says. "And call me if anything gets . . . weird."

"Ew, Dad." I climb out of the car, then duck back down into the open window. "And thanks."

The building in front of me, a one-story brown stucco structure with a concrete warehouse rising up behind it, looks about as far from Hollywood as I can imagine. There's no signage indicating that anything exciting is happening inside other than these bright yellow plastic things about the size of a piece of printer paper. They were scattered along the road starting about a half mile back, with black arrows on them directing people to various parking lots and the front door of the building. They each bear one word, all caps, in black, blocky letters: COLOR. I have no idea what it means.

All of a sudden my stomach feels like it's been pumped full of helium and is floating up into my throat. My hands shake a little as I lock my bike to a signpost, then hoist my bag farther up on my shoulder and go to drop my sunglasses inside, but I miss and they go clattering down onto the pavement.

"Chill out, Dee," I whisper to myself as I retrieve my sunglasses. "You're *supposed* to be here."

At least, I hope I am. There's only one door into the building, a plate-glass number with no signs. I don't know what I was expecting, but I was hoping for some kind of note saying, YOU! YES, YOU! THIS WAY TO CELEBRITY TIME! Or at least something marked RIALTO PRODUCTIONS.

I loop my bag over my shoulder and head for the door. As soon as I open it I'm met with a blast of arctic air-conditioning, a sure sign that whoever is here is not used to a south Georgia summer. There's a receptionist's desk just inside the small vestibule, but it's empty. There's only a hand-drawn paper sign with a shaky arrow on it pointing me through another door and down a hall. I check my phone. I've only got a few minutes before my call time, which, according to my Internet research, means the time I'm supposed to report to work, so I have no choice but to follow the mysterious signs.

Two steps down the hallway, I know I've arrived somewhere. I'm still not sure if it's the *right* somewhere, but it's definitely somewhere. No longer am I in a post-apocalyptic, deserted office building. The hall opens up into a spacious room full of desks and computers. All around me are people barking into cell phones or listening in on headsets, adjusting walkie-talkies clipped to their belts. A stocky blond girl in jeans and a T-shirt runs past me with a stack of papers in her hand, and I have to take a small step to the left to avoid becoming beige-carpet roadkill.

In the back of the office, I spot a familiar face underneath a Yankees cap. Rob is pacing about four feet of carpet, stomping hard with each turn. "You're kidding me! Again?" he barks into his phone. Then he slings the phone onto his desk, where it spins into the wall, and whips the ball cap off his head and flings it at the floor. "Dammit dammit *dammit*!"

I get the feeling that I'm not supposed to be watching whatever's happening with him, especially since everyone else in the room is doing that thing where they're very clearly *not* paying attention, so as he sinks into a rolling office chair and puts his head in his hands, I start looking elsewhere too. Finally, a woman who looks to be in her midtwenties sitting at the desk closest to me meets my eye. She's got a phone pressed between her ear and shoulder, a stack of papers in one hand, the other adjusting the volume on a walkie-talkie clipped to her hip. A cord dangles from a headset that's holding back her dark braids. She nods at me, so I just wait.

"Yup," she says. "Uh-huh. Copy. We've got the bus for first team, and I can get a couple twelve-passenger vans for the extras. . . . Yup. Day after tomorrow. Copy."

She hangs up, placing the phone and the stack of papers down on the desk in front of her.

"Are you Deanna?" she asks, pronouncing the "ann" with a long *a*. She stands up, winds a stray braid around her thick bun, tucking in the end, and then reaches out to shake my hand.

"De-ahn-na," I reply, the name sticking on my tongue like a wet cotton ball. My mother picked it, a shout-out to her Greek heritage, since she left her maiden name of Spyropolous behind. I've always hated it. Deanna. *Dee-ahhhn-na.* It's *so* not me. Deanna enters beauty pageants, gets regular mani/pedis, and knows all the lyrics to whatever cheesy pop song is hot that week. And while the pop songs are all me when I'm alone in my room, I've never worn heels and my nails are in shambles. "Call me Dee."

"Nice to meet you, I'm Carly." She steps out from behind the desk and starts down the hall, pausing only to wave me on after her. I have to skip a few steps to catch up to her frantic pace. She hangs a hard left into another small office and points to an empty chair. I sit like an obedient puppy, and she hustles behind the desk and sits down at a computer.

"Smile," she says, and before I can ask what for, there's a click. I hear the sound of an artificial camera shutter. "Spell your name for me?"

She types as I spell, then clicks on something with the mouse. A printer behind her warms up with a *whoosh* and spits out a white plastic card. Carly snatches it off the printer almost before it's done, then reaches into a box and produces a yellow lanyard with RIALTO PRODUCTIONS printed on it in black. She clips the card to the lanyard and hands it to me.

"Wear this at all times so security doesn't think you're some creepy fangirl and have you escorted off set," she says by way of explanation. I get a silent thrill from knowing I get to be in the building with a bunch of movie people and will *not* be considered a creepy fangirl. I slip the lanyard over my head while Carly rummages in a drawer, then slaps a piece of paper down on the desk. The form is packed full of hundreds of lines of teeny tiny text. "And sign this."

She tosses me a pen from the mug next to the computer. I catch it and sign, hoping it doesn't obligate me to shave my head or dance a jig anytime someone says the words "peanut butter." I slide the paper back across the desk. She takes it and slips it into a hanging file in the top drawer, which she closes with her hip.

"You can keep your phone on you, but on *silent*. Not vibrate. Not low volume. *Silent*. And no pictures of sets or actors or script pages," she says. "You do *not* want to be on the receiving end of Rob's yelling if he hears your phone or sees you taking unauthorized photos."

After seeing his meltdown in the outer office just moments ago, I believe her, and I decide it's probably best to keep my phone in my bag.

Carly heads for the door, and at this point I already know to follow without question. My heart is pounding a million beats a minute, so I try to calm myself with this fact. See? I'm already learning something. When Carly moves, *go*.

While we're walking, I take a moment to peek at the card. The top reads JUST ONE COLOR, which I assume is the title of the movie we're working on. Underneath is a grainy picture of me, my hair, which I've worn down, taking up most of the frame. You can barely make out my face in the technologically distorted image. I look like a Hobbit who's had a very hard week. Underneath that is my name, DEE WILKIE, and beneath that it says CREW. I can't suppress the smile that spreads across my face as I take it all in.

I don't have too much time to celebrate, though, because Carly is pushing through a set of heavy double doors into the cavernous warehouse attached to the back of the offices. It takes a moment for my eyes to adjust to the dim light, and even once they do I can barely see through the dusty haze of sawdust floating through the air.

"It's best to breathe through your nose in here, unless you want to be coughing up plywood for the next forty-eight hours," Carly says, shouting over the sound of a symphony of power tools buzzing and hammering all around us. She pulls the collar of her soft red T-shirt up over her nose and mouth, muffling her words. "They'll be done with interior construction in a day or two, so then it'll be fine."

I nod, squinting so I don't get an eyeball full of wood chips. She charges through the building, stepping over cables and boards and weaving around scaffolding. She checks over her shoulder periodically to make sure I haven't face-planted. And I might, because I keep taking my eyes off my path so I can take in all that's happening around me.

There are crew members everywhere in cargo pants and

heavy boots, thudding around with massive tool belts hanging off their hips. They're building what looks like a giant plywood pyramid dotted with a few windows. The walls rise a full two stories over my head. Through an opening, I see that though the outside is completely unfinished, the interior looks like an attic apartment, complete with worn wood floors and peeling wallpaper, an ancient-looking efficiency kitchen in one corner. It's like a life-sized dollhouse. A man inside is hanging a broken-looking iron chandelier from the ceiling.

"This way," Carly calls, and I realize I've stopped moving to stare. I jog after her to the back wall, where she's holding a door open for me. I step through into another warehouse room with soaring ceilings that looks like something that might be found in the basement of a museum. There are rows and rows of metal shelving extending high above my head. A rolling ladder leans up against one shelf in the back. Half the shelves are full of knickknacks and other items that I guess are props. Carly leads me to the middle row, where a short Asian woman, her dark hair pulled back in a severe ponytail, is lining empty beer bottles on a lower shelf, all of them affixed with labels I don't recognize.

"Dee, this is Ruth. She's our production designer. Ruth, this is your intern. Her name is Dee, and so far she doesn't seem to totally suck." Carly turns to me with a warm smile, as if she's just given me a ringing professional endorsement, and hey, I'll take it. "I'll see you later," she says, then disappears back into the warehouse.

Ruth dusts her palms off on her bell-bottom jeans and stands up, extending a hand to me. I notice that she's wearing a worn gray T-shirt with the Allman Brothers' *Eat a Peach* album cover on it. I want to ask her if it's vintage or a reproduction, or if she knows that the Allman Brothers recorded the album right here in Georgia, just a few towns north, but before I can ask anything, she says, "Ever done anything like this before?"

"Uh, no, ma'am," I reply, tugging at the strap of my bag. "They said I was going to be a runner?"

Ruth rolls her eyes. "This is a small production. Everybody is doing bigger jobs than normal, and that includes you." I'm shocked to hear that this, the warehouse and the construction and the crew of people running around, is considered a *small* production. What in the world does a *big* production look like? "You can put your bag right here," Ruth says, snapping me out of my wonderment. She directs me to a desk in the back that's stacked high with dinnerware, everything from plates to bowls to coffee mugs, all looking chipped and dingy, like they came from a thrift store. "We've got security, so it should all be safe, but still, don't bring your diamond tennis bracelet to work."

I take my bag off my shoulder and place it on the desk. "I don't have a diamond tennis bracelet," I reply, but the way she raises her eyes at me makes me realize she was probably joking. It's hard to tell with her deadpan tone, but I can tell that if I don't want to annoy her, I'd better figure it out quick.

"And none of that 'ma'am' stuff," she says. "I know it's the South and you're taught that crap, but we don't have time for politeness around here. There's lots to be done, and it needs to be done fast and right, so there's no need for niceties."

"Yes, ma—" The reflexive response catches in my throat, and I quickly swallow it down. I put my bag where she pointed, beneath a tall metal work table covered with stacks of paper and file folders.

"Welcome to props," Ruth says. Her voice is completely matter-of-fact, even as she sweeps her hand across the rows of shelving like a sarcastic game-show hostess. Then she shuffles over to the work table and pulls a stack of papers from the top, thrusting them at me. "Prop lists for our first on-location shoot. Pull everything listed here and pack it in boxes. *Carefully.*" She gives me the evil eye, and it's more than enough to make sure I handle everything on the list with all the delicacy of a curator at the Louvre. Before I can ask where to find boxes or if there are any other instructions, she mutters something into her headset, rolls her eyes, and disappears out the door.

Three

After two hours of pulling glassware from shelves and packing it into big plastic trays, the kind you find in restaurants and catering trucks, I'm starting to get the hang of Ruth's intricate system. I've been able to glean some of the finer details from her when she makes quick appearances in the prop room. I usually have time to get one question in, maybe two, before she starts muttering into her headset and disappears out the door again. But even without too much assistance, I'm starting to understand it, or at least fall into the flow.

Her inventories are all coded by scene and character. Everything I'm packing is marked "BG," which I find out means "background," which is what they call extras. The scenes are marked with roman numerals—we're shooting the first two scenes next week—and they both take place in some kind of space where drinks will be served, though I've been given no details about the actual scene itself. It's only my first day, but already production feels like putting together a thousand-piece puzzle when you're only given just ten pieces at a time.

"Don't forget the juice," she says, pointing to a case of sparkling apple and grape juice bottles. At first I wonder if this is going to be a scene set in a kindergarten, but after a few minutes of staring at the amber colors of the juice and the various bar glasses, I realize that the liquids will be standing in for alcohol. See? I'm starting to get the hang of this props business.

As I resume stacking pint glasses into the racks, I try to imagine them in the scene, but I don't even really know what the movie is about. I kind of thought my first day would be spent reading the script, but as I watch people dash around, their arms full of papers, cell phones and headsets glued to their ears, I realize how stupid that was. There's no time for anything quite so leisurely as reading. And I definitely can't ask Ruth. I'm pretty sure all I'd get is one giant eye roll. I guess I'll figure it out once we start shooting next week. Or maybe I won't figure it out until I see the thing in the theater. Or at the premiere. Do the interns get to go to the premiere? Probably not.

As soon as I fill a rack, I heft it, careful to lift with my knees (as Ruth barked at me during one of her lightning-fast appearances), and move it onto the top of a finished stack. I'm trying to keep the rattling of glass to a minimum. I don't want to know what the punishment is for breaking something, but I'm sure it can't be good.

The room has been mostly quiet. I'm tempted to pull out my phone, but I'm terrified someone will think I'm snapping a picture and have security toss me out into the parking lot. Ruth's the only person who's been in here with me, and that's only sporadically. Otherwise it's just me and the props. It's only been two hours, but already I feel at home here. Which is how I can tell immediately when someone new has entered. Maybe it's the lack of exasperated muttering or the fact that the echo of the new person's steps is slower than Ruth's hurried shuffling. And then the footsteps stop, and the back of my neck prickles and sends a little shiver up to my ears.

Somehow I know without turning around who it is.

"Uh, hair and makeup?"

The voice is deeper than I remember from our middle school dance parties, but it still matches all those soulful ballads and poppy hits. *It's him.* For a moment, nothing seems real. Not the racks of props or the papers in my hand. And definitely not Milo Ritter, who is standing in front of me looking lost and more than a little annoyed.

His face is the same one that's stared out at me from four album covers and countless magazines. I've seen those lips singing into the camera on TV and telling charming anecdotes on late-night talk shows. I've seen those dimples scroll by in GIFsets online and watched what must be hours of videos featuring those electric-blue eyes (not that I'd admit to still watching those). His face even stared out at me from my locker when I was in eighth grade, back when Milo had more of a long-haired-surfer vibe going on. I taped the picture up on the first day of eighth grade, just after his first album hit number one. I stared at it every time I opened my locker to find a textbook or hang my sweater, and it stayed there until just before winter break, when Aaron Eisenberg ripped it down, singsonging about how only losers listened to Milo Ritter. Even though the shaggy hair is gone, replaced by a closer-cropped do and the slightest hint of blond stubble, it's still unmistakably him. If nothing else, those piercing blue eyes give him away.

But back in the real world, where I'm not having fond memories of practicing kissing on a poster of Milo Ritter (not that I did that . . . but I totally did), I blink at the real-life Milo Ritter. I think he's asking me where hair and makeup is, but what comes out of my mouth is "Oh my God you're Milo Ritter."

Smooth, Dee. Real smooth.

As soon as I hear those words, all strung together and loud, I reach up and cover my mouth with both hands, my eyes going wide and, I'm sure, my cheeks turning crimson.

"Left down the hall, third door on your right," Ruth says, running in behind him. Other than answering his question, she barely takes notice. She couldn't care less that she's just brushed past one of the most famous pop stars in the known universe, even bumping his shoulder as she goes. She just hustles over to where I'm standing, takes the stack of inventory papers out of my hand, and shuffles through until she's found whatever she's looking for. She plucks that page from the stack, crumples it up, and tosses it toward a trash can in the corner. Then, just as quickly as she arrived, she's gone.

The silence returns to the room, but Milo is still there. He's looking at me like I've got something on my face, and it's only then that I realize what it is. It's an embarrassing expression of shock and awe, my mouth hanging open, my eyes wide. I blink at him. Now would be a good time to pull myself together. To not look like a complete and total fangirl/stalker/psycho. But it's not happening, and his nose is wrinkling now, taking on a look of faint disgust.

"I, um, sorry?" I say. My tongue trips over the words, not even able to get out one half sentence correctly. My God, I am such a goober. *Stop staring, Dee. Stop staring. Right now. Look. Away.* And finally—*finally*—I tear my eyes away from him and look down at my inventory sheets.

I hear a sigh and the sound of a long, slow stride retreating. Then the door opens and slams shut, echoing in the room, now empty except for me and an army's worth of glassware.

As soon as he's gone, all the blood that I didn't realize had left my brain floods back. I feel sort of like I might fall over into my tower of pint glasses. I throw a hand out to steady myself while my mind immediately begins to punish me, running me back through the last minute and a half of pure embarrassment, over and over again on a loop. Any hope I had of being cool—hell, of being *normal*—has completely disappeared. Milo probably thinks I'm a small-town loser, and right now it feels like he might be right.

The door swings open, and my blood runs cold. I'm worried it might be Milo again, back to hear me mangle the English language some more, but it's Ruth. She takes the inventory sheets out of my hand, the whole stack this time, and tosses them onto the work table. Then she thrusts a spiral-bound black notebook at me. I recognize it immediately. It's the exact same sketchbook I have in my bag in the back of the room, the same kind I've been using since Mrs. Fisher, my art teacher, first gave me one freshman year. This one is brand-new and covered in plastic, the hard black cover free of scuffs, the black spiral binding lacking any bends or chips. The white pages between the covers are crisp and bright, and I know if I held it to my face I could inhale the earthy smell of new paper.

"Go beat this up," Ruth says, as if that's the normal instruction that accompanies a brand-new sketchbook.

I blink at her. "Excuse me?"

"Beat it up. Make it look worn." Her tone is clipped. That's one question, one answer. I can *maybe* get one more out of her before she either dies of exasperation or simply walks away.

But I have *so many* questions. "How . . . I mean, are there tools? Or should I—"

Ruth shakes her head, a quick, tiny movement, like she can't believe she's having to explain this to me. "Go outside, throw it in the parking lot, drop it in some dirt, walk over it a bit, whatever. Run it over with your car if you have to. Just make it look like it's been carried around for the last couple years. It belongs to our main character. He's never without it, and it needs to look like it."

They're the most words she's said to me all in a row since I got here, and I mentally grab hold of them and hang on for dear life. I rewind them and run them back while she disappears out the door.

Outside it's blazing hot, and the gnats are almost as thick as the pollen. I sneeze and swat in front of my face before I remind myself that the trick with gnats is to blow them away. This is why I could never be a camp counselor. The outdoors and I do not agree on a whole lot.

With the sun beating down, the black covers of the sketchbook heat up in my hand. It won't be long before the spiral binding is collecting enough heat to leave a temporary brand on your leg, a lesson I've learned sketching through many Georgia summers.

A brand-new sketchbook like this one is something that usually fills me with excitement and a sense of possibility. Will I fill it with variations on a theme? Will it be a catchall for whatever flies through my mind? Will anything inside it turn into a bigger project? Leap from the thick white pages onto a canvas, or carve its shape into some clay? I never buy a new sketchbook until I have only one page left in the old one. It's a rule I made for myself long ago, partially to save money, and partially so I wouldn't wear out the feeling that comes with handing over $19.99 and bringing it home, of writing my name, email address, and "Reward If Found" on the inside front cover.

It all started when I was little, and my mom was on deadline for her first book, the kind of bodice-ripping romance novel she'd soon become famous for. I wanted to write books "like Mommy," but I was too young to know many words, much less spell them, so Mom gave me a coloring book and a brand-new box of crayons. When I'd filled every page, she started handing me blank pages from her printer, and when I started going through those too fast, she gave me old marked-up drafts so I could draw on the back of the pages. She says my art obsession grew out of her need to distract me without turning to the television. Whatever the reason, "making pictures," as I called it back then, soon became my favorite pastime.

When I started school, art class was my favorite. I loved everything I tried, from drawing to painting to collage. Even forming shapes out of gray lumps of clay. By middle school I was painting sets for the school plays and helping my teachers with their bulletin boards. I doodled in the margins of my notebooks and on every chalkboard I came across.

I didn't really care about being good at it. In fact, the thought barely occurred to me. It was just something I enjoyed doing, and my chief priority was doing it as much as possible. Sort of like my dad and running. I don't think he's ever entered a race, but he still loves his daily three-milers. Being the fastest, or even just fast, doesn't seem to matter to him at all. It's about going out every morning, lacing up his running shoes, and putting one foot in front of the other. For me, it's about pencil to paper, brush to canvas, hand to clay.

But then high school started, and everybody sorted into their groups: athletes, drama kids, school nerds. Everybody had a thing, and so art became mine. I was the girl who took every art class, and when she ran out, she started taking them again. Soon it wasn't just an identity, but a path. A future. Shows and competitions and the possibility of art school, maybe even a good one like RISD or Pratt. And one of the steps on that path was the Governor's School. It was an achievement, and also a necessity. It would look great on my applications, after all.

It was *supposed* to be a foregone conclusion, all of it. Dee is the art girl. She's going to art school. That's that. It was never even a decision I remember making. It just *was.*

And then it wasn't.

Getting that rejection letter didn't just knock me off the path, it drop-kicked me into the next county, and I'm still trying to figure out how to get back. Or if I even want to. Because staring down at this brand-new sketchbook, I don't feel anything. Not excitement. Not possibility. I feel as blank as the pages inside.

I tell myself that it's because this book isn't mine. I'm not supposed to draw in it at all. In fact, I'm supposed to treat this one exactly the opposite of how I normally treat my sketchbooks, which I guard from liquids and dirt and carefully close the covers with the elastic band to avoid bending the pages. This one needs to be exposed to the elements in a way that would normally make my skin crawl.

I wander around the parking lot until I find a patch of Georgia red clay, dusty and dry on the pavement. I glance around to make sure no one is watching this ridiculous exercise, and then I drop the journal into the dirt. A pink dust cloud rises up around it, but when I pick it up, all the dust mostly brushes off. Other than a bit of discoloration on the edges of the pages, the thing still looks brand new. So much for all that time I spent protecting my own books. Looks like this assignment is going to be a little harder than I thought. I'm going to have to get a little more rough with it, apparently.

I try again. This time I raise the journal over my head with both hands, then fling it down into the dirt. The dust cloud rises high enough to send me into a sneezing fit. Still, it hardly looks well worn, or even worn at all. So I pick it up and whip it like a Frisbee across the parking lot. It bounces and skids across the blacktop, landing with a spin. I run over and give it a decent kick with the toe of my boot, sending it farther across the ground. Then I chase after it, picking up speed and leaping at the last second so I stomp down on the cover hard with both feet.

When I look down at the sketchbook, now wedged beneath my feet, I don't feel blank. I feel *great.*

I don't know what comes over me, but suddenly I'm all about destroying it. I kick it and stomp it with such force that my hair starts to come loose from the messy bun I'd tied it up in. I can feel pricks of sweat forming on the back of my neck as I dance around on the cover, leaving footprints and scuffs.

"What did that thing ever do to you?"

He's made a joke, but the look on Milo's face is completely devoid of mirth. In fact, it's completely devoid of anything, like he's working overtime not to betray a single emotion. He's doing a damn good job, too. I have no idea how to respond. Despite his dour appearance, he's still totally smoking hot, with the blue in his T-shirt perfectly picking out the blue flecks from his otherwise stormy eyes. My cheeks go red and I feel twisty and nervous, like I should be cool and flirty but not flirt with him so he won't think I'm uncool. My mind is going in a thousand directions, and unfortunately it's just causing me to shift uncomfortably in my boots and toss my hair, which doesn't move because it's still mostly tied up in a bun.

In short, I look like a lunatic.

"I'm, uh—my job?" I say finally. So much for acting cool, or speaking in complete sentences.

"Mmmm," he says, nodding, and suddenly his appearance matters less to me than the fact that he's being sort of annoying. He's not giving me anything here. If he doesn't want a conversation, why did he walk over here? If he's going to stand there staring at me, he could at least participate. Be civil. He's acting as if someone is charging him by the word, and the price is steep.

I'm at a loss. "You want to try?" I hold out the book, which now has several scuffs and dirt-stained edges but still isn't nearly worn enough.

"No," he says, just like that. Just *no*, short and snappish in a way that makes me want to snarl at him, or at least roll my eyes. But I stop myself and drop the journal back into the dust. He stands there, staring first at me, then at the journal wedged under my foot. "Yeah, okay."

I blink at him, surprised. I take my foot off the journal, and he stoops down to pick it up. Without a word, he starts walking away with my assignment, over which Ruth may or may not kill me.

"Uh, hey, so—" I say, walking after him. I have to double my steps to keep up with his long stride. I follow him over to the grass off the side of the parking lot. As soon as he steps on it, he drops into a squat and grinds the edge of the journal into the ground until the edges of the pages are stained green, a few streaks of brown soil mixed in. He plants one foot on the edge for leverage and grabs hold of the other and yanks. The cover bends, forming a deep crease. Then he stands, strides over to a tree, a puny little newly planted one that's still being held up by stakes, and starts beating the journal into the narrow trunk. The branches of the tree tremble, and green leaves start raining down.

"Um, I think you're doing more damage to the tree than to the sketchbook," I say, and with his stony, sour mood I half expect him to whirl around and whap me upside the head out of sheer momentum.

He stops and glances down at the book. It definitely looks used, and *very* abused. His face a mask, he blinks at the cover, then thrusts it into my hand.

"Thanks?" I say, but I'm talking to his back. He's already halfway across the parking lot, headed back to the studio door.

The camera focuses on DEE as she squats in front of the fireplace in her house and ceremonially burns all remaining evidence of her Milo Ritter fandom.

Four

It's only a mile and a half from the studio downtown to Naz's house up on College Hill, but between the heat and my fury, I manage to work up a serious sweat. My shirt is practically glued to my back, and my bra feels like I wore it in the shower. The whole way there my mind is going over my run-in with Milo and coming up with awesome retorts to his totally jerkish behavior. If only I'd had the thought—and the wherewithal—to actually say them back then. Instead I stood there drowning in my awe of him while he treated me like something he stepped in. I feel embarrassed and pissed, a combination that's giving me a case of rage nausea.

When I arrive, I lean my bike against the whitewashed lattice of the Parad family front porch and climb the steps to the heavy stained-glass front door. I let myself into their sprawling Victorian, slip off my boots, and head straight up the curved staircase to Naz's room. She's got the bedroom in the turret, which, if I didn't already like her, would make me want to be friends with her immediately. I walk in and take a moment, as I usually do, to appreciate the vaulted ceiling leading up to the point of the turret. The round room, windows taking up almost 75 percent of the wall space, is small, but what it lacks in size it more than makes up for in character. We've played many games of pretend over the years where we took turns being badass princesses rescuing each other and fighting dragons (otherwise known as Luther and Watson, the Parads' ancient basset hounds).

Naz has all the windows open, as she usually does from the time the temperature breaks seventy in the early spring until the moment in the late fall when it drops again. The gauzy white curtains that frame every window are fluttering in the breeze, the leaves on the old oak tree outside rustling like a symphony.

Naz is at her desk, a hulking wooden thing that her mom saved from the Dumpster at the college. Her laptop is open, and she's *tap-tap-tap*ping away at breakneck pace. But one look at me and my angry red cheeks, my sweat-drenched shirt, and my shoulders heaving as I huff and puff from my bike ride over here has her clamping her mouth shut before opening it again to ask, "What in the hell happened to you?"

"He's a jerk! An ass waffle! A complete and total douche canoe!" I collapse back onto her fluffy bed as I spout my Mad Libs–worthy insults.

Roughing up the sketchbook was my last task for the day,

and I spent another hour with it after Milo left, channeling all my annoyance and frustration from his rotten behavior into the abuse of the poor thing. When I returned it to Ruth in the prop room just before I left, I earned a wide-eyed nod of approval. And I was too pissed to even appreciate it.

Naz stares for a moment, then cocks her head to the side. "I'm sorry, what now?"

Naz's parents are both Indian, from a small town just outside Delhi, but she was born squarely in the middle of Georgia, which gives her a slight Southern twang. It's a bit incongruous with her dark skin, almond-shaped eyes, and the long dark hair she keeps perpetually braided down her right shoulder, but it works for her. Naz is nothing if not incongruous. She's also incredibly hard to ruffle, and walks around like a tiny adult. I guess that's what happens when you're the youngest of six by a good four years. Naz's oldest sister, Divya, is in her late twenties and already has two kids of her own, four-year-old twin terrors who are as a cute as they are loud.

"Milo Ritter. I met him today, twice, and both times he treated me like, God, I don't even know what, but it sucked."

Before Naz can respond, Dr. Parad pops her head into the bedroom. She's got Naz's long dark hair, only hers is streaked with gray in a way that looks like it must have been professionally done. She's the most beautiful chemist I've ever seen. She teaches at Wilder, along with my dad and the other Dr. Parad, who both teach in the history department.

"Dee, are you staying for dinner? I'm making samosas."

Dr. Parad's veggie samosas are so good I have dreams about them. She uses English peas Naz's dad grows in their backyard garden. They're sweet like candy and so fresh they burst on your tongue.

"If that's okay," I reply.

"Always, you know that," she says, and disappears back out the door. As soon as it closes, I fall back onto Naz's bed and sink into the ruffles of her down comforter. I let out a sigh that's equal parts relaxed and annoyed.

"What do you care?" Naz says. "I mean, it's not like you're really going to be spending a lot of time with him, right?"

"No, but . . . I mean, he should be *nice*." Already my explanation sounds thin, because the truth is I was actually hoping to see a lot of Milo Ritter. My ears burn as I realize I was hoping to more than see Milo Ritter, like some ridiculous fanfiction fantasy. *Ugh, so embarrassing.*

Naz rolls her eyes. Even though I didn't say it out loud, she's known me long enough that she can probably tell. "Don't worry, it's not you. He's probably in some kind of deep, dark, broody depression over the whole Lydia Kane situation."

At this, I perk up. "What Lydia Kane situation?"

"The pictures," she says. I shake my head. I have no idea what she's talking about. "Lydia Kane cheated on him with some dude. Maybe a director? A producer? I'm not really clear on how those are different jobs, but it was some Hollywood guy."

Now I'm sitting bolt upright. "Where did you—I can't believe you know that!"

"I can't believe you *don't*," Naz says. And she's not wrong. Of the two of us, I'm much more likely to be up on the celebrity gossip of the moment. The DailyGoss is part of my usual morning Internet circuit, along with checking the weather and scrolling through SocialSquare to look at all the artfully edited photos of people's outfits and what they had for lunch. But two weeks ago I spilled a jar of paint thinner on my laptop, and my parents refuse to replace it until closer to the start of school in the fall. And since I hate reading on the tiny screen of my phone, I've been mostly Internet-free ever since.

Naz reaches over to pull her laptop from her desk and quickly types into a search bar. Immediately the screen is filled with a list of increasingly hysterical news stories about the scandal, all with little thumbnails of the offending photos. Naz clicks on the top one, which is accompanied by a dire warning about Milo's impending emotional destruction. The photo fills the screen. It's sort of grainy, but it's unmistakably Lydia Kane. And the man standing behind her, his arms wrapped around her waist, kissing her neck with what may be an errant pixel but is most likely tongue? Yeah, that's unmistakably *not* Milo Ritter.

"Oh my God," I mutter, my eyes moving over the text of the story. It happened two weeks ago, but the images came out only a few days ago. The man turns out not to be a director *or* a producer, but a lowly camera guy working on Lydia's latest film. No statement from Lydia, and no statement from Milo. In fact, the only image of Milo that's been captured since the photos came out is one of him barreling through a sea of photographers at LAX before boarding a flight to Atlanta to begin production on his first film.

It boggles my mind that I have a more recent sighting of Milo Ritter than the DailyGoss or any of the press. And oh could I tell a tale about it. Naz is right; he's apparently in a deep, dark place, and he's taking it out on whoever is unfortunate enough to come across his path. Which, today, was me.

"So they're broken up," I say, as much to myself as to her. I'm letting the information sink in, because Milo and Lydia have been a *thing* for almost as long as I've been paying attention to gossip. In fact, I barely remember a Milo before Lydia. Shortly after he burst onto the scene with his first album, a slew of singles, and a collection of smoking-hot videos, he met Lydia and they became a unit. They were the perfect pair: he a teen pop idol, she a teen screen starlet. It was sort of surprising that they managed to stay together as they both grew out of those identities. Milo's music took on a different sound, and Lydia's movies got darker and more obscure, and yet still they appeared on red carpets together and in countless paparazzi shots—pumping gas, buying coffee, grocery shopping, or simply trying to hide. But those days are over, apparently.

"I mean, nobody's confirmed the breakup, it seems, but I certainly wouldn't stay with someone after that." Naz clicks on the photo so it fills the screen, and my annoyance with Milo starts to fade, replaced with a growing sympathy. It must suck to count on a thing for so long, only to find it yanked out from underneath you.

Actually, I *know* that sucks.

"Poor Milo," I say. And now those images that were hiding in the back of my brain are starting to creep out, the ones of us eating lunch together, of us laughing on set, of . . . maybe more. They were pure fantasy, practically science fiction, when I thought he was still with Lydia. But now? I feel a small smile start to form, the corners of my mouth tugging upward. I bite my lip, which does nothing to hold in the massive grin that's now there. Sure, he was a total jerk to me, but now I know why. And eventually he'll get over it, and then maybe . . .

"Oh no," Naz says.

"What?"

She stands up from her desk chair and comes over to take a seat next to me on her bed. She pulls one leg underneath her so that she's facing me, and places her hands on my shoulders.

"Dee, can we have a moment of friend talk?"

I nod and brace myself for what will follow. "Friend talk" is the term we came up with for when we need to be honest with each other, even if it might sting. Declaring friend talk means the other person has to take a deep breath and not freak out about what the other person is going to say. The last time we had friend talk, it was because Naz was so busy studying for her AP chemistry exam that she neglected sleep, hygiene, and anything resembling nutrition. I caught her eating a lunch consisting only of leftover packets of oyster crackers and a flat, day-old ginger ale. It was *not* okay.

Naz takes a deep yoga breath, pulling her hands up, and then letting them float down to heart center with the release. It's a patented Nazaneen move that comes just before she puts on her most grown-up voice.

"Dee, I know you're having a hard time right now, and I suggested you needed a distraction—"

"I do!" Naz silences me with a stern look and one long, thin finger held in my face. "Right, friend talk." I clamp my mouth shut and mime a lock and key for added effect. Naz rolls her eyes but nods.

"I said you needed a distraction, but you're on the first step down a path toward a total lobotomy," she says.

When she doesn't expand, I jump in. "What are you talking about?"

She takes another deep breath, and then out comes the voice of her mother. "The dumbest thing you could do this summer would be to fall all over yourself chasing after some overexposed pop star who may or may not be heartbroken. It would be a distraction for sure, but not the good kind. And I can see from that look in your eye that you're already planning your outfit for your first date."

"Jeez, Mom," I say, my voice light to hide the fact that her words have hit a little close to home (my favorite broken-in jeans and the gauzy yellow top with the little ties on the straps). I flop back onto her bed, and she falls back next to me, both of us staring up at the apex of her turret.

"Dee, I know you. You are a person with a lot of . . ." She breathes in, searching for the right word. "Well, a lot of *feelings*. And sometimes those feelings can take on the properties of a heat-seeking missile."

"What does *that* mean?"

"Remember Ryan Burke?" I can't see her face, but I know she's cocking an eyebrow at me right now.

"Low blow," I mutter. Oh, I remember Ryan Burke, he of the black jeans and the wallet chain, who skulked around last year muttering about his graphic novel and shaking his shaggy, dyed-black bangs out of his eyes. He was a year ahead of us, but because it's a small town and small school, I'd known *of* him for years. And one day, while we were going through the lunch line, I experienced some kind of mysterious lightning bolt. I can't explain it, but all of a sudden I saw Ryan Burke in a whole new light.

"You followed him around for weeks until you finally worked up the courage to ask him to a movie," she says.

"Which was a disaster," I reply, nodding. When my best friend is right, she's right. I dated Ryan Burke for the entire month of October, culminating in a horrific Halloween incident where he took me to a poetry slam in Atlanta and got so stoned he forgot who I was and left without me. Naz had to make the hour-and-a-half drive up the interstate to get me, because I was too scared and embarrassed to call my parents.

"Ryan Burke is the reason you still have six black T-shirts in your wardrobe and a stack of comic books on your shelf."

"Graphic novels," I reply, thinking about the unread works of Alan Moore that at least *look* pretty cool alongside my collection of vintage art books.

"See? Who *cares* what they're called. You're never going to read them, but you just *had* to have them because all you could think about was Ryan Burke. And if you don't watch out, you're going to find yourself in some other ridiculous disaster spending your whole summer pining for Milo Ritter."

My cheeks burn, partly out of embarrassment and partly out of shame. I nod and sit up, pulling my knees to my chest and wrapping my arms around them to pull them tight. My eyes are on my feet, where royal-blue polish is chipping off my right big toe.

"You're right," I say. I meet Naz's eyes, and she's nodding right along with me, a sympathetic smile on her face. That's another thing I love about my best friend. She's so confident she's right that she doesn't have to gloat. I fling my arms around her neck and hug her, tears pricking my eyes. "I'm going to miss you this summer," I say, my words muffled in her hair.

"I'll miss you too," she says, then pulls back. "But if you need me, I'm only a text away."

INT. PARAD FAMILY DINNER TABLE.

DR. PARAD

So who is this Milo Ritter person?

DEE AND NAZ (singing)

Fast girl, you never go slow
You come find me and get real low
Red lips, soulful eyes
Can't stand to think of any goodbyes

THE OTHER DR. PARAD

That's music?

NAZ

Not the way I sing.

DR. PARAD

That's going to be trapped in my head
all night, isn't it?

DEE

Maybe days.

THE OTHER DR. PARAD

Oh dear God . . .

Five

At this moment Naz is in the backseat of her parents' Prius cruising down I-16 en route to campus, ready for the summer of her dreams being a science nerd with her fellow science nerds from around the state. Simultaneously, my fellow art nerds are convening on campus, ready to art-nerd their little hearts out without me.

And for the first time since my rejection letter arrived, I kind of feel like I don't care.

I tried my best to follow Naz's advice, I really did. But as soon as I crawled into bed last night, my brain kicked into overdrive. Suddenly I was imagining Milo onstage accepting a heavy golden statue and thanking me while I beamed up at him from a red velvet theater seat (wearing a killer couture ball gown, of course).

I know. I'm pathetic.

It's a cool morning, and I hop on my bike and get pedaling quickly so I can work up a little heat in my legs. It won't last, though. The forecast is calling for another blazing-hot day, with the temperature rising steadily through lunch. At least I don't have Dad driving me. I told him in no uncertain terms that having him drive me to work each day made me feel like I was getting dropped off at day camp. He agreed, but flatly denied my request for a family car to take. It's not like my parents are going to need two cars at home. Mom is a writer and spends most of her days wandering from room to room, carting her laptop and trying to make the cushions of whatever chair she's fallen into mold to her lower back so it doesn't spasm. And since Wilder College doesn't offer a summer program, my dad spends his days alternately working on whatever research he's been sucked into or putting miles on his running shoes on the long back-country runs of Holland County. Despite that very well-presented argument, if I do say so myself, I'm still stuck pedaling through the heat and humidity.

My wheels bounce over the railroad tracks as I turn onto the avenue toward the studio. There's no bike rack that I can see, so I pull up next to a No Parking sign and lock my bike to it.

Behind me, I hear tires squealing. A shiny black sports car, the same convertible that pulled up in front of the Coffee Cup last week, skids into an open parking spot. The door flies open, and I expect to see Rob step out, but it's not Rob.

It's Milo.

It's weird that they're driving the same car, but I guess if you show up at the car-rental counter and tell them you want the Hollywood Special, that's what you drive away with.

I don't realize that I'm staring at him until he glances my way and narrows his eyes. I can't tell if he's squinting into the sun or shooting me a death glare. He shakes his head slightly, then disappears inside the studio door. I try to give him the benefit of the doubt, remind myself that he's heartbroken, but it's hard. He's being kind of a jerk. Which may just save me from the romantic lobotomy Naz warned me about.

I wait a beat before heading in so Milo doesn't think I'm following him and give me another signature dirty look. Once I'm satisfied that I won't run into him, I head inside.

Carly sends me back to props, which she also tells me will be my home until further notice. I assume "further notice" is until I do something that makes Ruth decide I'm totally useless. She scares me, but I like the challenge of trying to impress her. As I walk into the prop room, I decide to make it my mission to earn some praise—and maybe even an honest-to-goodness smile—from her before filming is over.

I spend the next two hours checking things off lists and packing boxes. It sounds mindless and boring, but I like it. It's something I can finish, something I can accomplish. It's not going to reject me. And by lunchtime, I've even leveled up a bit in Ruth's eyes. Or at least I think I have. So far an appraising look and a brisk nod appear to be her highest forms of praise.

When Ruth calls lunch and bolts for the door, I retrieve the lunch I packed for myself this morning. I make my way back down the hall, through the set, outer office, and lobby, all of which are completely empty. Everyone seems to have gone out for lunch today. Outside I head to the picnic table where I ate lunch yesterday, take a seat in a spot that looks mostly free of bird poop, and unpack the brown paper bag. It's not much. We're in desperate need of provisions at the house, but Mom is deep in deadline mode on the sequel to her new novel, the first of which comes out in two weeks. She's doubly stressed because apparently this book is different from what she's written in the past, but that's all I know because as soon as she starts talking about writing her books, I start tuning out. I made the mistake of cracking the spine on one of them a few years ago and ended up flipping directly to a page that contained way too many euphemisms for male anatomy. I'm no prude, but no one likes to imagine her mother writing *that*, so I mostly stay out of it.

All that means I'm going to have to remind Dad that he's on grocery duty. Otherwise it's going to be cheese-and-mustard sandwiches all week. And not even good cheese, just two limp squares of individually wrapped "cheese product" that I found in the back of the deli drawer of the fridge. I try not to think about when we actually *bought* those singles as I take a bite of my sandwich. It's not what I would call good, but it'll do. Turns out all that packing and moving and stacking will work up an appetite for just about anything that can legally be sold as food.

A car door slams behind me, startling me and sending a bit of cheese product down my windpipe. I cough and gag, knowing in my head I need to chill out and take a breath but unable to convince my body to actually do it. I feel tears springing to my eyes as my coughing fit grows, and that sense of panic that wells in your chest when you're wondering where your next breath is going to come from.

There are footsteps behind me that I can barely hear over my wheezing, and then a hard slap on my back, followed by another. The shock of it stops my coughing long enough that I can get a breath in through my nose. A bottle of water appears on the picnic table in front of me, already open, and I grab for it and toss back a gulp. I feel the bite dislodge, and then I'm able to get a good deep breath.

"Oh my God, thank you." My voice is hoarse and scratchy from my near-death-by-cheese-product moment. I turn and see a tall shadow backed by the sun. It takes a minute for the tears to clear from my eyes before I recognize my savior, all tall, dark, and broody.

Milo.

"You're welcome," he says. He stares down at my sad sandwich, the little baggie of tortilla chips that contains mostly the broken bits from the bottom of the bag, and one carrot, peeled and chopped into thumb-sized bites. He grimaces, as if he's caught me eating out of a Dumpster. "Why are you eating that?"

"Um, because it's all I had at home?" What I really want to

say is, *Why are you judging my lunch, you pretentious prick?* It's a sentiment I'm glad I'm able to keep to myself.

Milo reaches down and sweeps my entire lunch into a pile in the center of the table, then wads it up and tosses it into the nearest trash can.

"Hey! What the hell?" Granted, it wasn't the greatest lunch in the world, but it was *food*, and it was *mine*. We can't all have personal chefs or reservations at whatever restaurant is hot at the moment.

"Come with me." He doesn't wait to see if I'm going to follow, just assumes I will. He's halfway across the parking lot in a few long-legged strides before I'm able to shimmy out of the picnic table and follow him back into the studio. I'm at his heels through the lobby and the main office, which is completely deserted. *Where* is *everyone?*

When we get to the end of the hall, instead of going through the warehouse, where set and props and everything I know is, he turns left down another short hallway that dead-ends in a pair of fire doors. He leans into one of them and it swings open.

The first thing I notice is that *this* is where everyone is. I see Ruth at a table in the corner, and Carly at another table laughing with a bunch of other people her age. The guys who were building the sets are all at another table, their tool belts hanging off the backs of their chairs. And at the table against the back wall, I see Rob sitting with an older woman with thick black glasses and wild curly hair. They're leaning in having a very intense conversation, Rob tapping hard on the table with his index finger, his mouth turned into what is becoming a permanent frown.

The second thing I notice is that the room is filled with delicious smells, salty and sweet, smoky and spicy. I don't think there's a single cheese-and-mustard sandwich in this entire room.

"Come on," Milo says, a few paces ahead of me, so I follow him to the end of what turns out to be a buffet line. Rows and rows of silver chafing dishes are set up on folding conference tables laid end to end. Yummy-smelling steam is rising up from pans of barbecue, wild rice, baked beans, some kind of seasoned vegetable medley—and that's just the first few trays. The tables go on and on, the entire length of the back wall. My stomach growls.

"I didn't bring my wallet," I say, wondering if I can find my way to props and back before I fall over from hunger.

Milo rolls his eyes, then gives me a look like maybe the air supply was cut off from my brain during my choking attack. "It's craft services," he says, with a don't-you-know-anything shake of his head. "It's free?"

"Seriously?" My voice squeaks a little, maybe because my mouth is spontaneously watering at the realization that I'm going to get to load up a plate.

Milo nods. "Yup. You work, they feed you. It's part of the deal."

"Crew too?"

"Crew too."

"Wow," I say. I follow his lead and pick up a heavy plate and some silverware. "I thought we worked, and they paid us. *That* seemed like a pretty good deal."

He gives me a side eye, but I swear I see the hint of a smile, the tiniest glimmer in his eyes, just enough to make my breath catch in my throat. But it quickly disappears, his face rearranged back to the blank expression I've grown used to. He turns back to the food. He scoops some of the pork onto his plate, then moves down the line adding coleslaw and baked beans and a warm, fluffy roll.

I make my way down the line, which is long and impressive. There's a makeshift salad bar filled with fresh, brightly colored vegetables and an array of dressings; an overflowing basket of warm, yeasty bread; and at the end, the pièce de résistance: an entire table of dessert. There are fresh-baked chocolate chip cookies and tall slices of layer cake, chocolate and carrot and red velvet. There are brownies and lemon bars and some kind of granola-looking thing, and it all looks absolutely amazing. It takes all the restraint I can muster not to pile my plate with one of each. Instead, I take a plate with a piece of chocolate cake, and at the last second also take a lemon bar, which I attempt to hide underneath my napkin so I don't look like a total glutton.

When I reach the end of the buffet, my plate perilously full and balanced on one hand, I look up, but Milo's gone. A quick glance around the room tells me that he's not at any of the tables, either. He just . . . left. I feel disappointed, and also embarrassed that I let myself think, even for a moment in the back of my mind, that he might be waiting for me. What, like, we were going to hold hands and skip to a table, sit down, and tell each other secrets over lunch? Please. Yes, he rescued me from sad cheese-product hell, but that was apparently just charity, and it wasn't like he was falling all over himself to help me. He did a nice thing, but he certainly wasn't very nice about it.

I shake off any lingering disappointment, aided by the memory of yesterday, when he treated me like something he'd stepped in, and make my way to an empty table near the front of the buffet line. As I take a seat, the only person in the room sitting alone, I can't help feeling like the new kid on the first day of school, only I ate my lunch in a bathroom stall because I didn't even know there *was* a cafeteria, much less where to find it. I probably could have gone to sit with Carly; I doubt she would have turned me away. But she and the other PAs are laughing and joking, loud and in the shorthand that comes from the kind of close quarters you find on a film set, even after just a few days. It feels impenetrable, and it makes me miss Naz like crazy. I unwrap my silverware and tuck into my plate of food. I choose to focus only on the fact that while I may still be eating alone, at least it's not a disgusting homemade lunch.

But I'm not alone for long. A few minutes later, a guy sits down across from me. I recognize him from my whirlwind tour yesterday. He was hauling what looked like lighting equipment and rigging through the warehouse, but that wasn't what made him stick out in my mind. Nor was it his bushy beard. It was his outfit: khaki cargo shorts, worn and frayed, and a purple T-shirt, with matching purple knee socks and a purple bandanna tied around his head. He's wearing almost exactly the same outfit today, only everything is green instead of purple. While he digs into his own plate, a small smile playing around the fringes of his ample facial hair, I give myself a second to stare. Did he lose a bet or something?

He doesn't say anything, so I don't either. I try to act like it's no big deal, like strangers in oddly color-coordinated outfits are just drawn to me, no bigs, but the word "what?" is hanging out on the tip of my tongue. After a moment, he drops his fork on his plate, where the clatter disappears in the buzz and chatter of the room. He pushes the plate back a bit, crosses his arms on the table, and leans forward, staring at me. Hard.

I glance over my left shoulder, then my right. Then I look down at my white tank top, a laundry-day choice, to see if maybe there's a trail of barbecue sauce running all the way down to my jeans. It would not be unheard of for me. But no, miracle of miracles, I haven't spilled on myself. Not yet, anyway. Something is *definitely* up.

"Uh, can I help you?" I ask, trying my best not to sound rude.

Beardy's face remains serious, then a smirk creeps onto his lips. "You really don't recognize me, huh?"

Wait, what? I study him. The buzzed hair and beard ring no bells, nor does the weird, color-coordinated outfit. But now that he's said something, there *is* a glimmer of recognition. Just a flash. I squint and tilt my head, trying to look past the beard to find the familiar face.

When he realizes I'm totally stumped, he breaks into a smile, and then I see it. The tiny gap between his two front teeth. He used to scare Naz and me by spitting a white Tic Tac into his hand, ketchup smeared across his lip, pretending he'd knocked out his own front tooth.

"*Benny?*" I say, loud enough that the crew members at surrounding tables turn to gape.

He laughs, the same belly laugh I remember hearing from down the hall at Naz's house. "It's Ben now, but yeah."

Benny Orazi was best friends with Tariq, Naz's older brother. They were seniors when we were freshmen, and Benny was at the Parad house almost as much as I was. Back then he had shaggy hair that constantly fell over his eyes and curled behind his ears and absolutely no facial hair save for the patchy stubble that grew after a weekend sleepover. He was that sort of nerd who was so committed to his nerdery (supersmart, AP everything, and near-perfect SATs to boot) that he was actually kind of cool. Naz always said he was cute, but I never saw it. I think she was mostly attracted to the 5 he earned on the AP Physics exam. I hadn't seen him since Tariq's graduation party four years ago. His family moved away at the beginning of that summer, just before he started college somewhere north and east of here, and to be honest I'd completely forgotten about him.

"Holy crap, Benny Orazi! What are you doing here?"

"No, really, it's Ben now," he says, glancing around to be sure he's not about to get a new on-set nickname. "It's Dee, right?"

I nod. I wish I had realized he only barely remembered me before I barked his full name to a room full of people. Now I sound like a superstalker. "You're working here?"

"Yup, just graduated. Film major, which made my parents crazy, but at least I managed to score a job right away."

"You're a PA?"

"Best boy."

"And modest, too."

He laughs. "No, best boy is a title. I'm Cole's assistant." He points across the cafeteria to a tall, lanky guy with shaggy blond hair held back by a pair of sporty sunglasses. "He's the gaffer, and he works for Allen, who's the director of photography."

I blush at my novice mistake. "Oh, that's great."

"Yeah, he's awesome. Supertalented and crazy connected. I'm hoping if I can impress him, maybe work with him on a couple projects, I can really get a leg up."

"So that's what you want to do? Lights?"

Benny shoots me some serious side eye. "Okay, don't say it like that. *Lights?*" He mimics my wrinkled nose, which I hadn't realized I'd done. *Oops.* "I want to be a director eventually, but

I really want a good technical base. Lighting, cinematography, editing. I did tons of internships during school, which is how I got this gig in the first place. A lot of people make the mistake of diving right in, trying to direct shorts and indies and commercials and whatever else they can. I want to develop all the skills to make me well rounded and technically proficient before I try to take on a director role. I call it my secret strategy of success. I like the alliteration."

Ah, there's the Benny I remember. And yet even as he's saying what could possibly sound pompous or totally nerdy, his half smile, his easygoing demeanor, the lilt in his voice all serves to make him endearing. It's exactly how he got away with talking about physics or chemistry or Brit lit at lunchtime in high school without getting a wedgie on the regular.

"How 'bout you? You haven't graduated yet, right?"

I shake my head. "One more year."

"And then?"

I laugh, but it comes out sort of squeaky and fake. "That's the big question, isn't it?" I flash him a superfake, superforced smile, my eyebrows skyrocketing. I'm sure I look totally demented. "That's why I'm here, I guess. I'm a PA. Working in props."

"For Ruth?" Benny drops his voice to a whisper, glancing around to make sure she's not nearby. "Intense."

All around us, people are starting to push their chairs back, gather up napkins and silverware, and make their way toward the doors. Apparently lunch is over.

"Yeah. Speaking of, I should probably go." I wrap my lemon bar in a clean napkin and hold it gingerly in my palm before gathering the rest of my leftovers to toss. Next time I'll try to remember that my stomach is about one-tenth the size of my eyes. My mom would kill me if she saw how much food I'm about to throw away.

I stand, my chair sliding back across the floor with an ear-piercing shriek.

"Well, I guess I'll be seein' ya," he says with a lazy two-fingered salute.

"Yup, later, Benny!" I say. He raises his eyebrows at me. "I mean Ben. Later, Ben!"

On my way out of the cafeteria, I whip out my phone and fire off a text to Naz.

Benny's back! He's working on the movie

Shut up. Is he still hot?

I wrinkle my nose, but then take a moment. I mean, he's not really my type, and the facial hair is a little much, but he's definitely better-looking. From the way his shirt was stretched across his chest, the sleeves tight around his biceps, it looks like all that hauling equipment on film sets has filled him out a bit. I guess if you like quirky and smart and funny, then yeah. So I text back.

Maybe a 4 on the AP Hotness exam?

INT. THE WILKIE FAMILY KITCHEN.

MOM

What's the movie about?

DEE

I don't know.

DAD

Who else is in it?

DEE

I don't know.

MOM

When does it come out?

DEE

I don't know.

DAD

What *do* you know?

DEE

When someone is drinking wine on-screen, it's grape juice in the glass. And craft services is for everyone, and it's free, and it's *awesome.*

DAD

Well, as long as you're learning something.

It's Friday, the end of my first week working for Rialto Productions. The week has been all about preproduction, finalizing details and schedules so we can start shooting on Monday. In my little world of props, we're packing items up by scene so they'll be ready for our first shots. It's been a week of packing and stacking. A week of amazing lunches and snacks from craft services. And a week of keeping my eye out for an ever-elusive Milo Ritter.

I haven't seen him since our not-quite-lunch. I'm not sure if he's been hiding in his trailer, brooding in his hotel, or if he's left town altogether until production begins. Or maybe he's hiding from me and my enduring awkwardness around him.

I hope it's not that one.

"Have you read the script?" Ruth comes bursting into the room with such force the door slams into the wall. Her braid is loose, her headset is askew, and she's got a stack of papers almost as big as her head balanced on one hand. On top is the sketchbook, looking decidedly more mangled than when she handed it over earlier in the week.

I shake my head, and she says, "Read it. I'm going to start having you do some more stuff with placement on set, and I'd like you to have a picture of the full story. Look for any place where there's a camera instruction to focus on specific items. Those are our responsibility. If you have questions, *ask*."

My power of speech is gone. Despite her hard edges, I must have impressed her somehow. Getting more responsibility from Ruth feels big. Huge. The sheer number of instructions she just gave me, at least twice as many as usual, tells me that.

"Script's in the red binder on the worktable. It doesn't leave this room, you got me? I see that red binder anywhere out there, it's your ass." She narrows her eyes at me like an executioner just waiting to drop the ax, if only I'd give her a reason. I nod, careful not to "yes, ma'am" her.

I expect it to take me all day to read the script. It's for a whole movie, after all, but it takes me only the better part of an hour. Movie scripts, it turns out, aren't that long and are mostly filled with white space, the dialogue squished into a column running down the middle of each page. Directions for lights and cameras and props and costumes run across the entire page, but even those are fairly brief. There's so much left unsaid, so much up for grabs. It's like a puzzle made up entirely of edge pieces, and the director gets to fill in the middle. I can see why Benny wants to do it. It seems fun and exciting to be able to make all that up and shape the story.

The movie is called *Just One Color,* and it's about a poor young graffiti artist named Jonas (played by Milo) who finds himself thrust into the elite art world when a photo of one of his murals goes viral. There's a romance plot line, where Jonas falls for the daughter of an art dealer who subsequently screws him out of his newest piece. I flip back to the cast list at the front of the binder to see who's playing Kass, the art dealer's daughter, but the space is blank. The other two principal cast members are Paul Anderson and Gillian Forsyth. They're both indie actors, famous enough that if you saw one of them in the grocery store you'd probably whisper to your friend, *Hey, isn't that the actor from that movie?* But you might not be able to produce his or her name. Still, I can't help getting excited. Paul was in that movie where he played an aide to the president of France, and he's pretty smokin' if you're into middle-aged hipster dudes with salt-and-pepper hair. Gillian has mostly done movies about women having various midlife crises. There was the one where she was a single mom, and one where she was a federal judge, and one where she hunted space aliens and fell in love with her boss. The rest of the cast is listed there, though, mostly older indie actors whose names I recognize but whose faces I can't come up with. I make a mental note to do some Internet searching so I don't embarrass myself should I run into them around set.

Ruth appears in the prop room, a stack of eight-by-twelve

blank canvases in her arms. She dumps them on the work table next to the red binder and the sketchbook.

"I need you to fill these in. Scene seventeen." She nods at the script binder.

"Fill them in with *what*?"

Ruth whips out a small spiral-bound notebook from her back pocket and flips through until she finds what she's looking for. She reads from her notes. "Abstract," she says. That's all. Just *abstract*. Gee, and I was worried she'd be vague about it. "Paint and supplies in the back. Let me know if you need something that's not there."

I place one of the blank canvases on the easel and stare at it, but I stall out right away. My brain is devoid of all thought. I don't think I could even *spell* "abstract" if I had to, much less produce it. Suddenly the enormity of where I am and what I'm doing comes crashing over me. In the last five days I've been catapulted into an entirely different world with its own customs and language. I was flying completely by the seat of my pants, assigned to pack boxes . . . and now I'm apparently a professional artist. At my job. On set. *What is life?*

I can feel my heart beating hard and my palms starting to sweat, so I quickly close my eyes and focus on my breathing. I channel Naz and her calm voice from that time she made me do sun salutations with her out on our front lawn. My muscles were screaming and sweat was pouring down my face, but if I just focused on her voice, I found myself sinking into downward dog. So I try to recapture that now.

I breathe in deep, filling my diaphragm like a balloon, then release and relax. Breathe in, fill up, release, relax. I run through it a few times until I feel my heart slow from a sprint to something more like a fast jog. I let my thoughts wander back to my first day on the job. It was only a few days ago, but it feels like a few weeks. Already my life is so different from what it was when Rob's car pulled up in front of the Coffee Cup. I feel the weight of the lanyard on the back of my neck. I smell the sawdust floating around the empty warehouse. I hear the muted sound of a buzz saw working away in the next room. I see the man hanging the broken chandelier inside the giant dollhouse that first day.

I open my eyes and attack my paints. I grab all the cool, dark colors from the case and start squeezing them onto the palette, mixing with the brushes. Then I turn back to the blank canvas and take one more deep breath.

It feels like time disappears in the span of that breath, and before I know it I'm staring at four finished canvases with a fifth on the easel. There's paint streaked up and down my forearms and caking my hands. At some point I'd ditched the brushes and started using my fingers for a rougher, less refined look. Inspired by the attic set they're building just outside the door, I finger-painted a crude version of the peeling wallpaper pattern I caught a glimpse of through the opening. On the floor next to it is a canvas painted midnight blue with swooshes and swirls of beige, an interpretation of the sawdust floating through the warehouse next door. Next to that are three more, each covered in paint and definitely abstract.

"Abstract expressionism. Cool."

I recognize the voice immediately, but it's still hard to believe it's real and talking to me, so I turn to confirm. Yup, standing there in a pair of dark skinny jeans and a tissue-thin gray V-neck is Milo Ritter. His Ray-Bans are tucked into the V of his collar, pulling the shirt down just enough to give me a glimpse of the tan, taut skin of his chest. I feel like a frat boy staring like that, so I force my eyes to go anywhere but his chest. *Focus on the words*, I tell myself.

"It's actually more abstract *im*pressionism," I say.

He cocks his head at me, an unasked question on his face, and I send a silent thank-you to Mrs. Fisher for her insistence on the study of art history. I continue, "Abstract *ex*pressionism is devoid of representation, like Jackson Pollock, but this is meant to be slightly representational, hence abstract *im*pressionism."

Milo stares at the canvases, so I step back and try to take them in with his eyes. It's something Mrs. Fisher always encourages. When you're creating something, it's really easy to just be *in it*, but it's important to try to see it how an outsider would, because 99 percent of the time art is viewed without the artist standing there. *If your art requires an explanation, it's not done*, she always says.

"You sound like a MoMA docent," he says. I feel like he's mocking me, but I choose to ignore it.

"I've never been," I reply.

"To MoMA?"

"Yeah. I mean no," I say. This is the longest conversation we've ever had, and I'm still having trouble speaking. I take a beat, then try again. "I haven't even been to New York."

"Lucky," he says. His eyes are still on my paintings, but I can see he's not really looking at them now. His thoughts are somewhere else.

"Lucky? Seriously?"

He snaps out of whatever brain bubble he was trapped in. He turns his gaze to me, and his bright blue eyes nearly knock me over like they have magnetic properties. "What, you don't like it here?" he asks.

"I like it fine, but it's not New York. Or Chicago. Or Los Angeles. It's not even Atlanta or Nashville. It's quiet. And boring. Did I mention boring? It's boring."

"There's something to be said for quiet and boring. It must be nice to be anonymous."

"Uh, no," I reply, shaking my head at him. "You seriously think small-town life is anonymous?"

"Well, yeah." He shrugs.

"Tell that to Bryce Johnson. In second grade he wet his pants while wearing green shorts, and now—ten years later—anytime anyone wears green shorts they *still* get called Pee Pants. Bryce Johnson would be more than happy to explain to you how *not* anonymous small-town life can be."

I can't believe I've just said "pee" to Milo Ritter, or that I've told him the story of Bryce Johnson (poor guy). But I don't have to be embarrassed, because for the first time since I've met him, Milo's lips curl up into a smile. A real one, and it grows bigger, his lips parting to show off his perfectly white smile, and the next thing I know he's laughing. It's a real laugh, too, the kind where you try to hold it in but it escapes out your shoulders.

"Anyway, I can't wait to go to New York. I need some excitement in my life," I tell him when his laughter slows, but as soon as I've said it, his smile disappears. That blank expression, a mask if I ever saw one, is back in place.

"Excitement is overrated," he snaps, and I physically recoil, as if his words have reached out and slapped me.

Before I can respond, Ruth appears, huffing and sighing and shaking her head. "Everything is pushed, which sucks, but it's bought us an extra day," she says. She shoots a quick quizzical glance at Milo, then turns her entire focus back to me. She looks around for the sketchbook, which she finds where I hid it beneath the script binder, then holds it up. "You can work on this on Monday. I'm going to have Rob come look at these"—here she gestures to my canvases, but gives not a single hint as to her appraisal of them—"and I'll let you know what he says. You're done for the day."

I look over at Milo, but he's already turning on his heel and headed out the door. Whatever moment we had is gone. Whatever cracks formed in his facade, he patched them. He's back to being a walking black cloud, and that black cloud is walking away from me.

Seven

On Monday, I return to the prop room ready to attack whatever Ruth throws my way. But when I walk in, my canvases, which I'd left leaning against the wall to dry, are in a stack next to the easel. I pick one off the top and find that the one beneath is smudged and smeared from the one that was on top of it, and the ones underneath it all suffered a similar fate. Two of them are actually stuck together. They must have been stacked on Friday, not long after I left.

Ruth comes in behind me with a fresh stack of canvases. "Uh, yeah, so Rob came in to take a look, and he hated those." She waves her hand at the stack of canvases like it's a pile of hot garbage. My stomach does a somersault, my breakfast feeling like it's inside a salad spinner. I swallow hard to try to calm it, but I can't do anything about the itch I feel in the corners of my eyes, a sure sign that tears are imminent. I turn my head so Ruth won't see in case they start to spill over. "He wants you to give it another go. This time he wants more right angles and more primary colors."

If I weren't feeling quite so much like a puppy who's been scolded with a rolled-up newspaper, I'd tell her that this was information I could have used on Friday. I mean, this was just a simple assignment. I would have followed those instructions if I'd had them instead of wandering off after some ridiculous muse and then getting slapped down. I try to shake it off, but the feeling is hanging heavy around my neck.

I take a breath to make sure my voice won't waver. "Right angles and primary colors? So, more Mondrian?"

There's a pause, but I don't dare look at Ruth to see her reaction. I'm still just barely keeping my tears in. "Uh, sure. Whatever," she says.

I wait for the standard scurry of footsteps toward the door, the sign that Ruth's headed off wherever it is she's needed. As soon as I hear the door slam shut, I squeeze my eyes closed tight, letting the tears that have pooled there spill over and run down my cheeks.

I didn't even want this job in the first place. I wanted to spend my summer as far away from art as possible. That first day Rob had said "runner-type stuff." If I'd known I was going to have to draw, to paint, I would have run, all right. Far, far in the opposite direction. Towards SAT prep or that boring office job Dad suggested. Hell, I would rather have been a camp counselor, and I hate heat *and* the outdoors. For a split second I consider quitting. I imagine how good it would feel to walk out the door and away from the stack of ruined canvases forever. Reject them like they rejected me. But I can't do it.

Instead, I wipe my cheeks with the sleeve of my shirt, blow my nose into a scrap of paper towel from the work table, and then place one of the new blank canvases on the easel. He wants Mondrian? That I can do. And then if he hates it, it's not me. It's Mondrian, and that's definitely not my problem.

I work until half the canvases are filled, until I no longer notice the tangy, earthy smell of the paint. I have no idea how long it's been, because my phone is in my bag and the prop room is like a casino: no windows and no clocks. I lose all sense of time. It could be tomorrow for all I know.

With my fourth canvas half filled with primary-colored grids, I pause to roll out my neck and crack my knuckles, left hand and then right. I hear the door open and shut behind me, but it's not Ruth's telltale scurry. Instead it's the slow strut of someone much taller and more relaxed.

"Ripping off Mondrian?" asks Milo.

I experience what I can only describe as my emotions just grinding to a halt, then spinning their wheels, little dust clouds rising up as my anger grows. When they finally shift into drive, I whirl around so fast little droplets of red paint fly from my brush and spray both the canvas and the wall behind it.

"You should wear a bell," I snap.

His lip curls. "What's your problem?"

"What's yours?" I say, the words coming out all angles and sharp edges. I can feel my ears get warm and a snarl start to curl my upper lip. I get that he's going through something right now, so I've overlooked the dour attitude, the blank stares, even the flat-out rudeness. But to walk in here and insult my work? When I'm trying my best? When I'm just trying to do what's asked of me?

This must read all over my face, a whole novel opening with my snappish retort, because Milo recoils. The blasé mask he's been wearing since I first met him cracks a bit, but he quickly puts himself back together. His expression is impassive.

"I was just making conversation," he says with a little shrug, just a tiny movement, but I can tell it's a telegraphed effort. It's not coming naturally to him. No, he's having to *try* to be this much of a jackhole. And somehow that just makes me more angry.

I give him a big, obvious eye roll before staring him down hard. "No. You weren't. You were being snide. And rude. Which I'm coming to realize is pretty standard from you, but I'm done with it."

"I'm, uh—" He stumbles, the cracks in his mask now fully crumbling. I can see a bit of red start to appear in his cheeks, and he shifts from one foot to the other, his hands digging deep into his pockets. But I'm not looking for an apology. What I want is to be left alone.

"Why are you even in here?"

He's been fidgeting like a toddler in church, but then he pauses and looks up at me, blinking. "What?"

I sigh. "Props. Why are you here?" I gesture around the cavernous room, just him and me and rows of shelves full of inanimate objects. "There's nothing and no one here for you."

"Exactly," he mutters under his breath.

"What was that?" My voice rises in volume, so the question bounces across the polished concrete floor.

And then it's all gone. All the anger, the cool facade, the blank stare, and the snarl. He glances down at the toes of his shoes and shakes his head slightly.

"You want to know why I come in here?" He finally looks up, his blue eyes locking in on me. "For starters, there're no windows in here, which means I don't have to worry about someone peeking in, maybe pointing a camera. In here, no one suddenly stops talking when I walk into the room. In here, no one stares at me or gives me sad looks like I'm some abandoned puppy. In here, no one bothers me."

That's when I know for sure that the Milo I've seen this week is not the real Milo. Not even close. Yes, he's heartbroken, maybe even feeling the lowest he's ever felt. But even then he's had to work to be the impenetrable jerk he's been walking around as since I met him. There's nothing about it that's coming naturally to him. He's acting his butt off and filming hasn't even started yet.

But still, there's something missing, something he's not saying. There's something I'm not quite getting.

"Okay, but don't you have a trailer?" I ask.

His eyes drop back down to his toes, and his voice comes

out just barely above a whisper. "Yeah, but in there, there's just no one."

For a moment, there's not a single sound in the room other than the industrial air conditioning softly humming through the vents.

I take a deep breath and let it out long and slow. "I'm sorry," I say. "I shouldn't have yelled at you. I know you're, well, I . . ." I pause, not sure if I should acknowledge his paparazzi problem or not. I decide to go with not. "I'm just having a bad day, that's all."

He glances over my shoulder at the canvas on the easel, then appraises the three I've got leaning against the wall. Finally, his eyes land on the stack of discarded canvases from Friday, the ones he complimented. He sighs, his eyebrows knit together, his lips pursed.

"Me too. Bad week, actually. Bad *month*," he says. He dips his hands back into his pockets, his shoulders rolling in until it looks like someone's let the air out of him. "I need comfort food, and I think you do, too. Let's go."

I couldn't be more surprised if he spoke to me in Sanskrit while dancing the tarantella. And unlike the other day, when he marched off toward lunch without a word, this time he stops at the door, holding it open for me. It takes me a second for my feet to catch up with my brain, which is screaming, *Go! Go!* But eventually I drop my paintbrush into the cup on the table, wipe my hands off on a stack of paper towels, grab my bag from the floor, and follow him.

ANGLE: ON A PILE OF DISCARDED CANVASES.

END SCENE

ANGLE: ON DEE'S PHONE.

A text message from NAZ appears on the screen.

Pic of Benny. Make it happen.

And in case you need a reminder:

Disengage heat-seeking missiles

Eight

"So where are we going?" I ask as I click my seat belt and he shifts the car into drive.

"Just this place I heard of," he replies. We emerge from the industrial area into downtown, and Milo hangs a left toward Poplar Street like he's lived in this town his whole life.

We ride mostly in silence, since I'm apparently not needed for any directions. I try to keep my eyes forward, or out the passenger side window, but every few minutes I allow myself a sneaking glance in Milo's direction. I notice that despite the driver's seat being pushed all the way back to make way for his lanky frame, his knees still seem bent and cramped in the tiny sports car, and he's drumming on the steering wheel to a tune in his head. A million questions are running through my head.

Soon, we're pulling up beneath one of the live oak trees dripping with Spanish moss that line Poplar Street. The summer sun hasn't quite set behind the neat rows of downtown buildings, but the trees provide a nice canopy that makes you forget, for just a moment, that you're living in a giant sauna.

I fling the door open and start to climb out, but the low profile of the car plus my denim pencil skirt has me performing a Cirque du Soleil routine just to remain upright without showing off my underpants to the little old ladies power-walking by. I finally get myself to standing with one heave on the roof of the car and a slightly embarrassing grunt, but a rock that's kicked up into my sandal causes my knee to buckle and I pitch forward. I fling my hands out to catch myself before I face-plant on the curb, but Milo, tall and solid, interrupts my trajectory.

My hands are flat on his chest, and the rest of my body follows, pressing into him nearly head to toe. I breathe in the scent of detergent and cologne and something smoky on him, and I have to work to suppress the happy sigh that's just waiting on my lips.

I glance upward to see his sparkling blue eyes looking back down at me.

"You caught me," I say.

"Yup," he says, and suddenly my bones feel like they're made of my mom's homemade strawberry jam. Despite Naz's warning and my own resolve to not turn into a puddle of fangirling goo, I can't help it.

Swoon. Swoony swoony sa-WOON.

Steadying myself and pushing away from his chest is maybe

one of the hardest things I've ever done, other than having to run the mile in gym. But I do it, because I can't think up a proper reason why we should spend the entirety of our dinner standing in this parking spot pressed up against each other. And if I tried, I'd worry that he'd find me creepy and never want to hang out with me again.

Oh, but if I could . . .

Milo holds the door open to the Deluxe Town Diner, home of the best burgers in Wilder and my favorite place to eat.

"Wait, have you been here?"

"Uh, yeah, on my first day in town," he replies, not meeting my eyes. There's something zooming around in his head, but I can't seem to grab on to it, so I make my way through the door.

Despite being the absolute best restaurant in town, it doesn't look like much, that's for sure. Big windows, and booths running across the front that are covered in sparkly red vinyl, which I know from many trips is cracked and peeling. There are already a few early birds, all of them regulars, parked on the stools that sit beneath the counter. A craggy, middle-aged man in a trucker hat and jeans that do not quite meet the bottom of his Jimmy Buffett tour T-shirt is perched on a stool nursing a cup of coffee.

"Hiya, Roy," I say as we make our way past him toward my favorite booth. Roy owns the music shop on the far end of the square and lives in the apartment above it. Whenever he's not at the shop, he's here. And when he's not here, he's at the shop tuning pianos or polishing brass. He's as much a fixture at one place as the other.

"Hey there, Dee," he replies, never taking his eyes off his biscuits and gravy. In fact, no one pays a bit of attention to me or one of the most famous dudes in America walking through the Diner. That is, not until a blond head pokes out from the door to the kitchen, a big smile spreading across her lips. I can tell from the way her eyes get wide just for a second that she recognizes him, but she quickly adjusts her face so as not to betray anything.

"Well, if it isn't my best customer," the woman calls, her voice sounding a little like nickels in a garbage disposal. She wipes her pink-polished fingers on a well-worn apron around her waist. "You park your buns at the booth in the back, and I'll be right with ya!" And then she disappears back through the swinging door to the kitchen.

The booth is big and round and easily the most abused, with peeling duct tape covering the larger cracks in the vinyl. It's where Naz and I usually park when we eat here, because the table is big enough that we can spread out homework or sketch pads or the multiple plates of food we usually order. But because it's past the window line, tucked in the corner, it's a little dark, so usually no one else wants it. Which means we don't have to feel bad about commandeering it, even during a lunch rush.

I plop down on the seat and scoot around, Milo following behind me. Then I pluck two menus out from where they stand between the chrome napkin dispenser and a bottle of ketchup and hand one to him. He flips it open and starts scanning, while I lay mine on the table in front of me. I don't need a menu. If Milo weren't here, I wouldn't even need to order. Kristin knows my usual by heart: cheeseburger, no onions, add avocado, with a side of extra crispy fries and a bottomless Coke.

Milo notices my neglected menu and raises an eyebrow over the top of his.

"If you've eaten here, you probably know the burgers are the best you'll ever have," I say. I lean over and flip his menu, pointing at the center column. "But if you're looking for something with a little more local flavor, Kristin apparently makes the best pimiento cheese sandwich on the planet."

"Apparently?"

"She wouldn't know, because she's never tried it," Kristin says as she slides up to our table. She pulls the pen out of her bun, licks the tip, and holds it poised over her pad. She's grinning at me, her lips closed tightly like she's swallowed a secret and it's bursting to get out. Kristin inherited the Diner from her grandmother, who inherited it from *her* father, who opened the place back in 1920, though back then it was more of a soda shop. Kristin has updated the menu, adding Fluffernutters and smoothies and the best damn lentil soup on the planet for her vegetarian customers, but some things remain the same. And the pimiento cheese is legendary.

I grimace. "Pimiento cheese looks like something that's

already been eaten," I reply. I turn to Kristin and offer her a smile. "I believe everyone when they say yours is excellent, but no thanks."

Kristin rolls her eyes. "I know what *you'll* be having," she says to me before letting her gaze roam over to Milo. There's a sparkle in her eyes, and I can't ignore the hint of a hair flip when she turns to him. I don't blame her. "But what'll it be for your fella here?"

I can feel my cheeks give away my embarrassment, but there's no use fighting it. Kristin is Kristin, as I've come to know in my years eating at the Diner. She's never met an emotion she could hide, an opinion she could contain, or a person she wouldn't feed. She's got the biggest mouth and the kindest heart in Wilder. She's not quite old enough to be my mom, so she's always felt like the cool big sister I never had.

"I will have the pimiento cheese sandwich," Milo says, his eyes on me like a challenge, and Kristin laughs as she scribbles. He adds a water and a side of fries, a crooked smile playing at the corners of his mouth. I like this Milo, the one who can tease without taunting, the one who might even smile a bit.

"Girl, you got a live one!" she says, swatting at me with her order pad. She takes our menus and shoves them back into their slot by the napkin dispenser, then spins on her heel and beats feet for the kitchen.

With Kristin gone, Milo and I are left alone to stare at each other, and once again an awkward silence falls over us. But before I can open my mouth and say something 90 percent ridiculous, Milo's phone beeps.

And beeps.

And beeps again.

Someone is apparently texting him a novel one line at a time.

Milo reaches for the phone, and something stormy passes across his face. Immediately my brain goes to the DailyGoss and the endless links and photos about Lydia. I wonder if this has to do with that. I wonder if it's actually *Lydia* texting, but one look at his face tells me I don't dare ask. He clamps down on the volume button, lowering the ringer until it's silenced; then he shoves the phone into his pocket. And as if he can see the line of inquiry on my face, he dives into a conversation feetfirst.

"So, you seem like quite the regular," he says. It takes a moment for the sour expression to fizzle away, but it does, and soon it's replaced by the happier Milo I recognize from TV. I don't think Angry Milo is normal, but I have a sneaking suspicion that this Milo, Man of Sparkling Personality, isn't real either. We might as well be sitting across from each other doing a late-night interview or something.

"I am, but how did *you* find this place? It's amazing, but it doesn't really scream, *Hey, Hollywood, dine here.*"

Milo shifts in his booth. The vinyl squeaks, an audible indication of his discomfort. "Someone, uh . . . someone told me about it."

It takes me about point two seconds before the realization hits me like a glass of ice water to the face. The shiny black sports car. Rob and Milo don't have the same car. Rob was driving *Milo's* car. And the shadowy figure in the front seat, the one Rob kept glancing back at, was Milo.

Which means he heard . . . My mouth gapes as I try to fill the awkward silence, but no words come.

"I think the phrase you're thinking of is 'sucks out loud,'" he says. I can practically hear Naz's voice, haughty and sure as it always is.

"You heard that," I say, not a question, because I already know it's true.

"Yup," he says. He shrugs, giving a little shake of his head. His Sparkling Personality is cracking a bit, but he's holding on to it with a tight, wry smile. I can tell he wants to make a joke out of it, brush it off, but I guess Naz already took care of that. "Also, 'music to have a coma to.' I gotta admit, that was a new one."

I shift in my seat and purse my lips. "I'm sorry. About Naz. She doesn't always have a filter, and . . ." I try to come up with something to say that makes the whole thing not so harsh. I mean, stuff like that gets said all the time about celebrities; it's not like you really *mean* it. It's not about *them*, exactly. And it's not like you ever think they're going to actually hear it. And even if they did, they've got money and fame and all that, so who cares what some small-town nobody thinks? But now that I'm sitting across from Milo and watching him struggle to hide the cracks in his foundation, I realize it's not that simple. Or maybe it *is* that simple. Mean is mean, whether they're a million miles away or right in front of you.

"I'm sorry," I say again. No qualifiers, because it needs to be said.

"It's okay," he says. "I mean, I get it a lot. Not quite so often to my face, but definitely quite a lot on the Internet."

I shudder. I keep my social-media feeds private, because the idea of strangers popping in on my life totally freaks me out. But that must be what Milo's whole *life* is like: strangers raising their hands to offer up their opinions on his life. "I never thought of it like that."

"You're lucky," Milo says. "It's one of the less fun aspects of my job."

I laugh, and Milo raises an eyebrow at me in question. "It's just that you call it a job," I say. "I mean, teacher, doctor, lawyer, those seem like jobs. Waitress, bagger at the grocery store, traffic cop. It's weird to imagine a career day where you'd show up and introduce yourself as a worldwide teen pop sensation."

He grimaces. "Okay, first of all, if I ever use the phrase 'worldwide teen pop sensation' to describe myself, promptly direct me to kick my own ass," Milo says. And then there it is again. The smile, the *real* one, and a bit of a laugh. I want to whip out my phone and film it so I can watch it over and over again, but that's pretty much the exact *opposite* of what he wants or needs right now. "But it's definitely a job. It's work, anyway. One that never really stops, unless you want to disappear for a weekend to a private island."

Kristin drops our drinks and some straws on our table, and Milo spends the next minute or so fingering the wrapper, tearing it into tiny bits and moving them around on the chipped Formica table. Our awkward silence is finally interrupted by the sound of heavy plates landing between us, our food ready in record time.

"Dinner is served," Kristin says, an ancient floral dish towel in her hand acting as a hot pad. Her eyes dart between us, taking in our silence. "Don't talk too much, now. That food'll get cold."

"Thanks, Kris," I say. I give her a grateful smile, which she returns with plenty of warmth. I suspect if Milo weren't here with me, she'd bend down and wrap me up in a hug. Across the table, Milo tucks into his pile of fries, so I follow suit. My burger smells perfectly meaty, the lettuce and tomato towering on top, and I know from hundreds of burgers past that as soon as I smash the lid down on the bun, juice will run down onto the plate, and I'll be warm and full and happy. Such is the power of Kristin's burgers. They always seem able to chase away the bad days.

After a few minutes of silent—but delicious—chewing, I can't take it anymore. I'm actually watching Milo Ritter, whose face lived for a short time in my ninth-grade locker, dribble pimiento cheese onto his lower lip and then slowly lick it off. The sight of it sends a shiver down my spine. I'm pretty sure no one in the history of *ever* has looked that good licking food off his own face. I feel like I'm starring in a Milo Ritter music video, like at any moment he might pull a guitar out from underneath the table and sing about broken hearts over our plates of fries. The fact that this is my real life and not an elaborate fantasy I dreamed up while getting my wisdom teeth out is straight-up insane.

I've stared at him (and the spot on his chin that he just licked) for a bit too long, though, because now he's staring back, his hand holding his sandwich paused halfway to his mouth.

"What?" He reaches up and swipes at his mouth with the back of his hand. "Did I miss it?"

At that moment, the whole situation reaches a point so surreal as to be bordering on an episode of *Candid Camera,* and I'm pretty sure they don't make that show anymore. I slam my burger down onto my plate, the silverware jumping on the table.

"Can we have friend talk for a minute?" I stare right into his bright blue eyes, ignoring the acrobatics in my stomach.

"Friend talk?"

"Yeah," I reply. "It's a thing my best friend and I do when we want to avoid the awkward and just get to the root of it. You know, not beat around the bush."

Milo gulps like there's a stubborn bite of sandwich stuck in his throat. "Um, okay?" He puts his sandwich down, then folds his arms on the table in front of him as if he's preparing to give Senate testimony. I wonder when the last time he had something approaching friend talk. If the many faces of Milo Ritter are any indication, it's been a while. I imagine quite a lot of his life is carefully choreographed and scripted by professionals, so this is probably quite a leap for him. I'm impressed that he's going along with it.

I should probably think about this for a second, but if Naz were here she'd tell me to just get on with it. Real talk works best unfiltered, and let's be honest, filtering has never been my strong suit. So I dive in.

"This situation is weird, okay?" I gesture across the table, but I'm talking about more than the meal.

Milo cocks an eyebrow at me, and I can see that he has no idea where this is going. Which is fine, because I'm not really sure, either. This is going to be harder than I thought.

"I mean, it's fine, and you're very nice *now*," I add, giving him a pointed look. He seems to sink slightly in his seat at the reminder of his earlier bad behavior. "But you're *Milo Ritter.*" I watch him glance around the Diner quickly, then slouch farther in his seat. Not that he needs to. Not a single solitary soul heard me, and even if they did, I doubt Roy or Melanie over in the corner eating her daily chef salad while reading a paperback mystery cares a bit. "I'm trying to be normal and cool, but it's hard sitting here having dinner with a Grammy winner."

"Nominee," he mutters, picking at the toasted crust of his

sandwich. Little crumbs sprinkle off his plate and onto the Formica.

"What?" I lean across the table. Milo sits up straight.

"I have four Grammy nominations. No wins," he says. He picks a stray fry off the table and places it back on his plate before meeting my eyes again. "And things aren't exactly normal for me right now," he adds, his eyes now glued firmly to his plate.

"Okay," I reply. The running headlines and the string of photos sit heavy on my mind, but one look at his eyes, which are starting to cloud over again, tells me not to go there. Instead I head for the question I'm dying to ask. "Fine. Forgetting everything out there for a minute. Let's talk about this. Right here. And why, after being prickly and rude for a whole week, you brought me here."

He sighs. "First of all, I'm sorry for being a jerk. Like I said before, it's been . . . well . . . Things haven't been great for me lately. Not that it's an excuse." He glances up at me, his face full of apology. I nod to accept it, and he continues. "It was that weird pee-pants story. Honestly, you were the first person to make me laugh since . . . well, in a really long time. And you weren't trying to. You were just talking, not to 'worldwide teen pop sensation Milo Ritter,'" he says like the words taste sour. "Just Milo. Like I was anyone. I'd forgotten what that felt like. And when I saw you freaking out, I felt like I should return the favor. I mean, I wanted to."

Kristin appears at the table. I shoot her a look that says

Please go away, we're having a moment. She smiles apologetically, but doesn't leave.

"Dee, I hate to break up the party, but Drew over there says a gentleman just stopped by the hardware store looking for your friend here," she says with a nod of her head toward Milo. I turn and see Drew Walker, clad in coveralls fresh from the job site, leaning over Thelma's counter. The buttons on the material are barely hanging on over his ample stomach, a by-product of eating every one of his meals at the Diner. He's glancing our way, his face showing signs of triumph from having delivered some good intel.

"What kind of gentleman?" Milo asks. He sounds weary, like he already knows the answer.

"The kind with one of those cameras with a lens bigger than God," she says. She turns to me. "He's working his way down Poplar Street. Should be here any minute. If I were you, I'd go hang out by the dry goods until I can tell him where he can shove that camera."

Milo curses under his breath, then stands up. "Come on, Dee."

I'm temporarily frozen by hearing him say my name, but then the enormity of the situation hits me. Those grainy photos of Lydia? They come from situations just like this. Milo hasn't been photographed in weeks, and a shot of him post-Lydia will be *everywhere*, never mind a picture of him having dinner with *me*, a nobody. I've read enough DailyGoss to know how that would go. I'd get called a "mystery girl" in the headlines, and a target would follow me for who knows how long. It's the very thing that turned Milo into a misery monster, and I want no part of it.

I rise from the table and follow Milo behind the counter and through the door to the kitchen, pausing to look around when I'm on the other side. All these years of burgers at the Diner, and I've never once been on the other side of the counter, much less in the kitchen. I feel like I'm treading on sacred ground, but I don't get long to genuflect. Milo grabs my hand and drags me through an open door just off to the right. The pantry, which is about the size of my bathroom at home, is filled with cans of tomato sauce, chicken stock, and bags of sugar and flour. Milo nods at me. "In here."

I want to tell him it's okay to relax. We're safe back here. Only about three people in the Diner saw me with Milo, and none of them are talking. Roy barely says two words to anyone, and while Melanie can talk a blue streak, she's really particular about what she calls "outsiders." She'll say hi to me because I was born here, but she still shoots suspicious looks at my parents, New England natives who she refers to as Yankees.

Still, I'm not complaining about being in a confined space with Milo Ritter. A tasty meal *and* espionage with someone who recently sang on late-night television? Um, awesome. Granted, I got to eat only a few bites of said tasty meal, and the fine layer of flour that coats everything in here is making my nose itch. But it's far superior to what I would otherwise be doing right now, which is wandering around my house ignoring my sketchbook and wondering where my life went. I'll take hiding in the dry goods storage over that any day.

As soon as I squeeze in after him, I hear the bell on the door tinkle. There's a man's voice, but I can't make out what he's saying. The words "musician" and "magazine" drift through the doorway, but that's about all I get.

Milo leans over me, his ear toward the door. That's when I realize we are close. Like, *close*. The room isn't that small, but the abundance of products leaves very little space for two people to stand in here. While his attention focuses somewhere over my head, trying to listen in to the conversation out front, I take the moment to look at him without embarrassing myself. *Really* look at him, without getting caught, for the first time since he wandered into the prop room that first day.

I must have seen his face staring out at me a thousand times from magazine racks, TV screens, blogs, and billboards, but now I'm close enough to study him. I start with his face, going over the lines, contours, and quirks like he's a model I'm about to sketch. I notice that his left eyebrow has a little cowlick, so the hairs stand up at odd angles and make him look a little rascally. I notice two dark freckles marking his tanned skin, one under each eye, nearly mirror images of each other, the one under the right eye just a fraction of an inch lower than the one under the left. I notice the way his jaw, which looks like it was chiseled out of marble, tightens as he strains to listen for the reporter.

I keep studying him because I'm afraid that if I stop, my heart will start beating loud and hard, a one-man band going to town in there.

I hear more mumbling, but I still can't catch a word. Finally, Kristin's voice chimes extra loud.

"I'm sorry, but the most famous people in Wilder are up at the college. If Milo Ritter passed through here, it was just that—passing through. Probably on his way to Savannah. You should head down there," she says. A bit more mumbling, then the bell on the door jangles again. I start to back out of the doorway, but Milo grabs my arm, sending an electric current down to my feet that curls my toes. He holds up one finger and mouths, "One more second." I nod, not that I'm in danger of moving at all. I'm practically rooted to the floor, the rubber in my sandals melted there by the heat of Milo Ritter's chest. Then there's a knock at the door.

"All clear, but I'd leave out back if I were you," Kristin says. She hands me two Styrofoam to-go boxes with our meals in them.

"Thanks, Kris," I say. Milo gives her a quick hug, and she pats him hard on the back.

We end up in the alley between the Diner and the hardware store. Milo glances around like a CIA operative, but there's no one in sight. When he's satisfied that the coast is clear, he leans back against the brick wall and sighs. Now it's my turn to want to help him, but all I can come up with is "I guess we should probably call it a night?"

He nods. "Yeah, probably a good idea." He looks down the alley toward where his car is, and I can tell he's already nervous about what—or who—might be waiting for him down there.

"Hey, I don't live that far. I can totally walk home," I say.

He barely waits for me to finish before he's shaking his head, but I hold up a hand to halt his argument before it begins. "Seriously, I walk here all the time. It's not far, and to be honest, I don't want any part of whatever that was in there."

I can tell he doesn't want to let me walk alone, but my argument wins out over whatever sense of chivalry he has. He nods. "Okay. I'll see you tomorrow," he says, and though his voice is sad, there's a spark somewhere in my chest at the words. It's a connection, an acknowledgment of more, and I desperately hope for it.

There's an awkward shuffling where it seems like he might go in for a hug, but instead he raises his hand in a sort of half wave, half salute that makes me smile. I wave back, and we head off in opposite directions, out of frame of any lenses that may be watching.

The walk home takes a good twenty minutes, but I barely notice it. I'm practically floating. *I think I made friends with Milo Ritter.* The thought singsongs in my head the whole way.

When I get home, Rubix, our big old yellow rescue dog, is waiting for me. When we adopted him as a puppy from the shelter four years ago, they told us he was a yellow Lab. But then he grew and grew until we became convinced his dad was a Great Dane (that, or he was bitten by a radioactive spider that turned him part giant). He's absolutely enormous and as sweet as he is large. When he spots my takeout box, his tail starts thumping loudly on the wood floor. I flip the lid and offer him a chunk of my burger, which he swallows without chewing.

"Did you even taste it?" I ask as I ruffle his ears. I drop the to-go box in the fridge, then head toward my room. Mom's office door is shut, which means she's either hit her stride or she's in megaprocrastination mode and doesn't want anyone to know it. Either way, her closed door means *do not disturb*. And since the sun hasn't quite set yet, Dad is probably still out on his nightly run, which means I don't have to worry about either of the parental units noticing my blissful attitude.

I crash onto my bed with my phone for my nightly scroll through SocialSquare and a few of my favorite news (okay, gossip) sites. But tonight I'm so tired, I feel like I won't even make it halfway through before my eyes start to drift closed. Maybe it was the painting, or maybe the roller coaster of emotions, or maybe just the walk home. Whatever it is, I'm exhausted.

The first thing I see is a story about Moriah Mann, who's just been dropped from her supporting role in the latest Robert Lewin movie. Which is . . . Holy crap. I'm reading gossip about the movie I'm working on! I think back to the blank spot next to the name Kass on the cast sheet. Was that supposed to be Moriah Mann, *the* indie starlet? Her long blond hair and thin frame manage to make her look both like a supermodel and your very best friend next door. Her last movie got her a Golden Globe nomination, and everyone expects her to get an Oscar pretty soon. She's always seen skulking around New York or LA on the arm of one of many studly indie rockers with greasy hair. I read further to find she's off to rehab, so that must be what Rob's been freaking out about. All the stomping and yelling and hushed conversations are because she got fired, and they're trying to replace her after we've already started production.

Next I switch to SocialSquare and start flicking through my feed. I pause on a shot that Naz posted that looks like it's inside the library. The tabletop in front of her is arranged with a stack of books, notebooks, and pens all in perfect right angles. The filter gives it a hazy glow, and underneath is the hashtag #myhappyplace. I feel a swelling in my chest. I miss Naz, my favorite nerd. It's weird not having her around to talk stuff out. Texting just isn't the same. I want to call her, until I notice the second hashtag in the caption: #donotdisturb.

Instead, I flick my finger across the screen and watch as beautifully filtered images drift by. I once tried to make my feed look that beautiful, but it was so much work to edit and export and import and filter that I gave up. Most of the time

I don't edit at all, since my feed is mostly pictures of my own artwork. I use it as sort of a mobile gallery, with silly selfies of me and Naz or me and Rubix mixed in.

My finger pauses over an image of a blond woman wearing a flower crown made of pink peonies while standing in a field somewhere. It's Natalie Bond, who starred in a reality show about being young and fabulous in LA called *The Boulevard.* As I wonder who took the picture and how she came to be standing in a field wearing flowers on her head in the first place, a tiny itch of an idea starts forming in the back of my brain.

I wonder . . .

I click on the little magnifying glass in the corner and type his name in. It comes up immediately, and I click without thinking. His feed appears, and right at the top, the very first image, is a familiar-looking pimiento cheese sandwich. The second image is from almost three months ago, and the one after that from two months prior. He almost never posts. But there, on the tiny screen of my phone, is our dinner from earlier, taken from above. The shot is mostly his plate, but in the top left corner you can see the tips of my fingers, the teal polish chipped, with a few stray marks from the black grease pencil I'd been using at work to mark dishes for Ruth. There's the ring that Naz got me for my birthday last year, the brass bird that looks like it's about to take flight from my hand. I wear it almost every day.

The only caption on the image is a simple hashtag: #yum. Nothing about the movie or me, but still, it's a record of the fact that we were together. And it makes me feel giddy and slightly jumpy, and I do a little shimmy of my shoulders to try to let some of the excitement out. Suddenly, I'm not quite so tired. I click on Milo's avatar to load his full feed. A stream of photos appears, though he's hardly prolific. The most recent shot prior to today was from nine weeks ago, when Milo was standing onstage taking a crowd shot of a bunch of screaming fans—mostly girls about my age and their moms. Most of the other shots were taken inside a studio, from back when he was making his newest album last year. He appears in almost none of them. And because I can't help myself, I notice there aren't any of Lydia either. Not even her fingertips.

I click back to the #yum photo, my stomach instinctively growling even though I'm still stuffed. My eyes roll over every pixel of the image, as if there might be a hidden message or a clue in it, but there's nothing there. Still, I can't stop looking.

Until my eyes roam down past the photo to the comments below. In the five minutes I was looking at Milo's feed, the photo has already amassed more than five hundred likes and climbing, and comments keep pinging onto the screen. Most of them have nothing to do with the actual image. About a third are in a language other than English, and several are even spam advertising fan pages and places to buy designer handbags (CHEAP! AUTHENTIC!). But just before I close the app, I notice a new comment full of exclamation points and emojis, the kind of hysterical missive that you can hardly imagine an actual person writing. But someone did. Just now.

OH MY GOD DO YOU THINK THAT'S LYDIA????
OR IS IT SOMEONE ELSE????
MILO NO NO NO DATE MEEEEE!!!!

I grimace, feeling secondhand embarrassed for JAZMEENA 29384. But then another comment pops up.

THAT'S TOTALLY NOT LYDIA.
LYDIA WOULD NEVER HAVE SUCH UGLY-ASS NAILS.

It's followed by several comments speculating as to my identity, none of them kind.

And just like that, my stomach drops. My cheeks feel hot, and I find myself shifting uncomfortably in bed. There's a creepy-crawly sensation running up my arms and across the back of my neck, and before I can think anything of it, I'm climbing out of bed and pulling my shades shut, making sure they overlap so there's no space for anyone to look in. Then I double-check my own SocialSquare page to make sure it's still private. There's no way any of those crazies could find me. It was just my fingernails. Not even all of them. I'm still anonymous. Right?

I know I should brush it off. I should close the app and go back to my own corner of the Internet. I should do *anything* other than sit here staring at this photo. But even though everything in my head and the sick feeling in my stomach is telling me to put down my phone, I refresh the feed. The photo now has thousands of likes, and the comment thread is getting longer. Most of them are still of the fawning-fan variety, but there's also a growing conversation of sorts happening between a few people on the thread. They're trying to figure out who that manicure belongs to, and they're not very happy about the prospect of its being someone other than Lydia.

DEE

Mom, do you have any nail-polish remover?

MOM

No, but I can pick some up if you want.

DEE

Please.

Nine

The set is a totally different world when I arrive on Tuesday. Today is scheduled to be the first day of filming, and everyone is walking around like they're at the starting line of a marathon. The atmosphere is crackling with energy, just waiting to hear Rob call out, "Rolling!"

I check in with Ruth, who tells me I'll be spending the day shadowing her. I follow her into the warehouse to the attic set, where we'll be filming the first shot of the day. It's Milo's character's tiny studio apartment. It's a scene without any dialogue, just the camera capturing Milo puttering around the set. Ruth points to spot near a rolling cart filled with props for the room and tells me to stand there.

All around me, crew members are working busily like bees in a hive. Lights rise up on metal poles, fat electrical cords are hauled around, cameras are mounted on shoulders and dollies while one sits on a cart that rests on a little silver track.

I spot Milo in a tall director's chair. He's got the day's sides in his lap, and is going over the scene while a man adjusts his hair with a pick and two makeup women dab at his face. Behind him, a short woman is on her tiptoes adjusting the collar of his vintage button-down so it's sticking up slightly, as if it happened by accident and not very particular design.

"Okay, people, here we go!" Rob calls. He pulls on a pair of headphones that will allow him to hear what the boom mike is picking up, then positions himself behind a set of three monitors to watch what the cameras see. Immediately, the set clears as everyone takes up residence out of view of the three cameras. Milo steps onto the set and takes his place on top of a tiny X of gaffer's tape. He bobs up and down on the balls of his feet a few times, then rolls out his neck like he's preparing for a prize fight.

"Rolling!" Rob yells.

"Rolling rolling," the cameramen reply.

"Sound speed," he says.

"Speeding," the young guy hoisting the long boom mike replies.

"Action."

The set is quiet except for the sound of Milo's footsteps as he moves through the cramped attic set, and even those are dulled thanks to the layer of foam the sound guy stuck to his heels. Milo picks up a blank canvas that's on the floor and places it on an easel—my easel, from the prop room—then picks up a pencil and sweeps it across the white space. I glance at the monitors in front of Rob, and suddenly the Milo in front of me becomes Jonas. The lights and the wires and the tape marks on the floor are all gone, and it looks like an artist in his crappy studio apartment. You can't tell that the light streaming in through the windows is coming from an enormous lighting rig full of bulbs. You can't tell that there are approximately thirty people in the room. You can't tell that the apartment is missing its fourth wall, open for only those of us on the other side of the camera to see.

Now I know why they call it movie *magic*.

When Rob calls cut, the set springs to life again. Cameras move, lights are adjusted, and the hair-and-makeup team climb over cords and weave around cameras to meet Milo at his mark, fluffing his hair and dabbing his forehead. And it's now, while surrounded by a small army, that he spots me, still rooted to the floor by the props cart where Ruth left me. He lifts his chin and smiles as much as the makeup assistant will allow while she's working on him, but it's enough. I feel a warmth in my cheeks that has nothing to do with the hot lights all around. That's real the Milo looking at me, even as he's surrounded by people and dressed up as someone else.

"There's a box on the work table filled with books," Ruth says, and I have to break eye contact with Milo to turn to her. It's harder than I want it to be. "Grab it and bring it here."

And that's how I spend the rest of the day, running between props and set, often waiting outside the studio door until I hear Rob call cut, so I can enter without disturbing filming. I quickly learn to live in mortal fear of making any noise while the camera is rolling. I bring books, dishes, and boxes of knick-knacks, so Ruth can adjust things in the shot as Rob requests them. We replace one of the posters hanging on the wall of the attic, a vintage circus shot, because it's pulling too much focus. This is our chance to get the attic set right, since this is the first time shooting in it. From here on out, everything that comes in, goes out, or gets moved around will need to get documented with a tiny point-and-shoot camera that lives in Ruth's pocket, because everything needs to be in the right spot for every shot that comes after. Otherwise we'll start piling up continuity errors that will take the audience out of the story or wind up in snarky comments on message boards. It's our job to avoid that.

By the end of the day, I'm exhausted. My arms ache from carrying boxes, my feet ache from running and standing, and my ears are ringing a little from the cavernous silence of the set during filming. I can think of nothing but my bed, and possibly curling up with Rubix at my feet. And the rest of the week is the same. I learn to wear my most comfortable sneakers every day, partly for comfort and partly because they don't make any noise when I move across the concrete floor of the warehouse. I learn to leave my phone off and in my purse so I don't have to worry about remembering to silence it on set (this lesson came after a makeup assistant got a thorough reaming-out from Rob when her phone started quacking during a scene). Eventually, Ruth hands over the camera and puts me in charge of taking continuity photos. And by the end of every day, all I want is to fall asleep until I can wake up and do it all over again.

I don't see much of Milo throughout the week. During lunch, he's either in his trailer, rehearsing with Paul and Gillian, or going over the script with Rob to prepare for upcoming scenes. I see him plenty on set, but he's always surrounded by a fleet of people attending to him. The only time he's not surrounded is when the camera is rolling, when he's Jonas, and then I definitely can't talk to him.

By the time Friday rolls around, I feel like we've been filming for a month, not barely a week. Life on set feels like an alternate reality where time simultaneously flies and grinds to a halt. Maybe it's because we spend so much time recreating tiny moments from different angles and with slightly different inflections. Hours can pass, but on camera it's only been a few minutes.

Rob has just called a wrap on the day, and I'm piling items back onto Ruth's cart to return them to the prop room when Milo appears. The skin on his arms is red and scrubbed tattoo-free, and he's out of his punky Jonas wardrobe and back into his standard relaxed jeans and V-neck T-shirt. I haven't seen him out of wardrobe in days. It's amazing what clothes can do. He's *him* again, the version I want to see.

"Hey," he says.

"Oh, hi." I realize that I'm trying to sound casual to hide the fact that I'm staring at how good he looks in that dark-green shirt. But I'm failing. Miserably.

"I never did get a chance to say thanks. For having dinner with me last week."

"I think I should be thanking you," I reply. I can't believe it's been a week since the Diner, and that I haven't talked to him since then. It feels like a lifetime ago that I was crying over the paintings in the prop room. "You were the one who was pulling me out of my funk."

"Well, I just wanted to tell you that I had a good time. It was nice to get out. I've basically spent all my time either here or in my hotel room watching basic cable. I'm pretty worn out on reality TV and home improvement shows at this point."

"You should get out. See the sights," I say. Across the studio, Ruth gives me a look, and I know I need to get the cart back. I may be leaving for the day, but she'll still be here for a few hours packing boxes and getting ready for next week, when we'll be on location. I start pushing it toward the exit, and to my surprise Milo falls in step with me.

"Well, I was thinking, I don't really know what the sights even *are*—so since you're from here, maybe you want to hang out this weekend?"

I stop walking, and the cart squeaks to a halt. I blink at him. "Seriously?"

"Well, yeah," he says. He slips his hands into the pockets of his jeans, his shoulders rising slightly in a shrug. "But maybe someplace not supercrowded?"

I immediately think of the SocialSquare comments and hiding in the dry goods storage. I remember how Milo's eyes darted around the alley before he slunk off toward home. So far only my fingernails have experienced that kind of public paranoia (and they've since been scrubbed clean of chipped polish, as if they've joined the manicure version of the Witness Protection Program), and already I don't want anything to do with it.

"Uh, that sounds great," I say. "And absolutely."

Milo lets out a breath, like he was worried I might say no, which is completely and totally upside-down ridiculous, but it's cute that he doesn't think so. "We should probably be careful. You know, about being seen together," he says. He shuffles his feet, and a cloud of sawdust kicks up around the toe of his boot. "Not that there's anything to see. But, uh, now you've seen how crazy things can be. So, you know, we should watch out."

"Yeah, of course," I reply. I'm shocked that now *I'm* the calm and collected one, while he's playing the role of stuttering nervous guy. "Tomorrow morning? Say around ten?"

"I'll do the driving, you do the navigating?"

I shake off the comments that are still pecking at my brain and smile. "Sounds like a plan."

Ten

"We'll be back late," Mom says, leaning against my doorframe. "Call if you need anything, and if it's an emergency, call the doctors Parad. They're in tonight."

Early this week, Mom started to get that twitch in her left eye that we all know means she needs a break from writing. When Dad saw it at breakfast this morning, he told her they were going to drive up to Atlanta for dinner at their favorite sushi restaurant, whether she wanted to or not.

"If I have to kidnap you, I will," he said, taking a sip of his coffee out of his EITHER YOU LOVE HISTORY OR YOU'RE WRONG mug. "But my knee is acting up, so please don't make me resort to that."

For the first time in days, Mom's out of her office and her favorite purple yoga pants. Dad very wisely picked a restaurant with a dress code, so she's wearing a pale-blue sundress; her curls, long and brown like mine, though streaked with gray, fall past her bare shoulders. The bunny slippers I bought her as a joke three Christmases ago have been replaced by a pair of brown leather sandals.

"Lookin' good, Mom," I say.

She rolls her eyes. "Any plans for you today?"

If I tell her that Milo Ritter is picking me up to hang out and see the sights in Wilder, I'm afraid she and Dad will never leave. And as much as she needs this night out, I need Mom and Dad not to give the world's biggest pop star the parental third degree.

"Just a date with some laundry and a *Paranormal Diaries* marathon," I tell her.

"Team Salinger," she says, declaring her allegiance to the muscled werewolf from our favorite TV show.

"Ugh, no way. Team Auden," I reply. I prefer the tall, dark ghost hunter.

She laughs and shakes her head. "Always with the bad boys."

As soon as I hear their tires pull out of the driveway, I leap off my bed and fling open my closet doors, pulling out my favorite butter-yellow top, gauzy with little ties at the shoulders. After I've thrown on a pair of worn cutoffs, cuffed just above the knee, and my gray leather sandals, I study myself in the full-length mirror on the back of my closet door. It's too hot for my favorite jeans, the ones I imagined wearing when I pictured our first date back at Naz's house, but I think the outfit is a good mix of fancy and relaxed.

Not that this is a date, of course. Just two new friends hanging out. No big deal. No need for my skin to feel cool and tingly. No reason for my heart to be pounding out a heavy bass rhythm. No reason for the manic grin that keeps trying to take up residence on my face.

Ugh, those damn heat-seeking missiles.

I spend a moment reminding myself about the Internet commenters and the telephoto lenses and Milo's broken heart, which helps calm the tingles and the pounding, though there's nothing to be done about the grin. He's not even here yet, and already my cheeks ache.

When Milo arrives to pick me up, his tiny black sports car has been replaced by a big, shiny black pickup truck. It's like his baby car finally grew up into a big-boy car. The truck is one of those giant diesel numbers, and the *chug-chug-chug*ging of the engine makes it sound like you could hitch our whole house to the back and haul it up to Atlanta with minimal effort.

"Where's the Audi?" I ask as I skip down the path toward the truck. I hope I don't sound too snobby, because I really couldn't care less about cars. All I care about is that it has four wheels and an air conditioner, and really the four wheels are negotiable. It's my parents who have made me take a blood oath never to get on the back of a motorcycle.

"This is way more practical," he replies. He opens the passenger door for me, and I climb in. The door slams behind me, then Milo makes his way around the front of the truck to the driver's side.

"For all those major construction projects you've got lined up? Camping trips up the summit of K2?"

"And to blend in a bit," he says. "The Audi was way too easy to spot."

Milo turns on some music, a singer-songwriter I've never heard before, but I hear only a few notes before the music fades away. We drive with the windows down, sneaking smiles at each other, the roar of the wind covering the music and preventing a whole lot of conversation, which is pretty fine with me. When I'm done giving him directions to the two-lane country highway, I settle in for the drive, leaning slightly over the center console. I can smell the earthy, sweet scent of his cologne, or maybe just his detergent in the thundering wind that swirls through the truck's cab.

"You gonna tell me where we're going?" he calls over the rush of the wind.

"Just keep driving," I reply. I tuck a strand of hair that's escaped from my ponytail back behind my ear and watch the rolling hills and grassy fields rush by as we cruise down the two-lane country highway.

His eyes fixate on the road in front of him, a smile playing at the corner of his mouth. "I like the sound of that."

We drive for just over an hour, but the minutes fly by. I'm tempted to give him bad directions so we can get lost for a while, because I can't think of much better than just sitting beside him. But when I spot the mile marker that signals our turn is coming up, I direct him to slow down and take a left at a crumbling brick gate flanking a dirt driveway. The truck bounces over long-worn ruts in the road, off to the side of which is an ocean of pecan trees in perfect staggered rows as far as the eye can see. They're ancient, with wide trunks and long branches creating a canopy over the land. The temperature drops slightly as we're shaded from the beating sun, and the breeze feels even more heavenly. By August, it'll be unbearable out even in the shade of the trees, but in early June it's the perfect summer oasis.

Farther down the road, massive live oaks, growing since before the Civil War, line the way and overtake the ordered view of the grove. The branches twist and gnarl and lean over the road as if weighed down by the gray tangles of Spanish moss that drip from the branches. At the end of the dirt road, the trees part for an overgrown lawn and a hulking behemoth of a ramshackle old mansion.

Milo pulls the car around on what was once a circular driveway, throwing the truck into park at the front entrance. He leans his head out the window, taking in the sagging veranda, the shutters hanging crooked by rusty bolts, and the front door with the stained glass panel, now dusty and cracked and sporting one tiny bullet hole in the top left corner.

"What *is* this place?" There's a bit of awe in his voice, which is carried away on the breeze. It's how I felt when I first found this place—how I *still* feel every time I see it.

"This is Westfell Grove. It dates back to before the Civil

War, and once upon a time it was rumored to be a stop on the Underground Railroad."

"It looks like it should be a museum."

"It should, or at least a historic site, but the guy who owns it is a crook or maybe just a jerk. Either way, he's decided it's too expensive to restore, so he's letting it rot." The long-since-forgotten property hasn't had a tenant in at least fifty years, and the house shows it. The white planks of the siding have grown gray with mildew and moss. The bottom-floor windows are all blacked out with plywood so old it's actually starting to peel off the house, and several of the second-story windows have been broken by pecans or rocks or worse, sent flying by roving vandals. The whole house has settled over the years, but unevenly, so the porch sags on either end, making the house look like it's frowning.

"Wait, this is private property?" Milo ducks his head to peer through the windshield, looking for some security guard or homeowner with a gun to come screaming up to us, but none does. "Aren't we trespassing, then?"

"Yeah, but the owner lives up in Atlanta. I don't think he's been down since he bought the place. He's just waiting for it to fall down so he can avoid the hassle of paying to have it demolished. He's probably *hoping* we'll vandalize it." I've heard my dad go on and on about the tragedy of demolition by neglect, especially when it comes to historic sites. That's how I first found Westfell. I was in middle school, and Dad and I were playing one of our epic games of Which Way Does This Road Go? Our only rule is to obey all No Trespassing signs (*Those people have guns,* Dad always said), but this place didn't have any. Which meant not only did we drive right up to the front door, but on later trips we even discovered a place where the plywood was falling off and crawled inside to do some exploring. It was Dad who discovered the rumor about the Underground Railroad, and he's spent part of his summer research every year trying to substantiate it.

If I can find proof, I can save this place, he always says, wistful but determined, like some sort of historic-preservation superhero. I want it saved, too, but there's also something about the way it looks now, almost sagging under the weight of its history, that I like.

"Maybe we should trespass and do some guerrilla maintenance," Milo says.

"A noble thought, but this old girl needs way more work than a hammer could do. Basically it needs to be gutted, reinforced, and top-to-bottom restored." Now I'm pretty much quoting my dad word for word. I make a mental note to thank him for dragging me along on these trips, even when I was an unwilling participant (in my defense, sometimes a twelve-year-old would rather stay home and find out who's getting told to pack their things and go on whatever iteration of bad reality TV competition happens to be on at the time).

Milo's eyes rove over the bones of the house. "It's so sad.

You can just barely tell what it used to be. It's almost too far gone to imagine."

I pull out my sketchbook from my bag. I'm still carrying it around out of habit, but now it's going to be of use. I flip a few pages. "You don't have to imagine. Here it is." I visited the county archives in the basement of Wilder City Hall last summer with Dad to find the picture. Ever since I first saw it, even in grainy sepia, I couldn't stop drawing it. And that was when I started coming out here by myself whenever I could convince my parents to let me borrow a car. It became my secret place, my muse, and I have a whole stack of sketchbooks back in my room with more drawings of the property. Sometimes I'd bring Naz with me, and she'd settle onto one of the low tree branches and watch a game or study for an exam. But I haven't been out here since I stopped sketching. Standing here in front of the house feels like visiting a friend you've been neglecting. I'm excited to see it, but sad that it's been so long, embarrassed that I dropped the ball.

Milo flips the page to where I've done a pencil sketch. On the left side of the paper, the house as it was: shutters straight, sun glinting off the glossy paint, blooming azaleas lining the wide porch, which has all its spindles lined up straight like tin soldiers. But as Milo's eyes move across the page, the house deteriorates into the leaning, hulking structure in front of us, like someone is wiping away the past.

He holds the sketchbook up so he can eye it in line with the reality of the house in front of us. "You did this?"

All of a sudden I feel shy, an emotion I hardly recognize. I've never been precious about my artwork before. My parents used to have to negotiate with me over how much time I could spend showing my artwork to their dinner-party guests. Otherwise I'd have been like the kid at the piano, banging out tunes over the conversation while the guests tried not to roll their eyes.

"Dee, these are incredible."

He flips through similar sketches of the house from various angles, even one of the oak tree we're standing under. It's the only part of the property that's flourished over all these years. The branches have expanded out as if they're attempting to hug the yard, and they're positively dripping with gray Spanish moss, giving the tree the appearance of an aged lady looking after the place. I could draw that tree until the sun goes down, and then capture it by the moonlight. And suddenly, it's all I want to do. My fingers twitch at my side, longing to reach for a pencil for the first time in weeks.

Milo turns the sketchbook back around so I can look at my own work. "You're really talented," he says.

And just as fast as it arrived, that need, that *drive* to draw is gone, replaced by the doubt that has been my constant companion for weeks.

"I'm okay," I say, but I'm not talking about my talent, nor am I telling the truth.

The snap of the covers on my sketchbook brings me back.

Milo offers it to me like it's an act of mercy. I take it and stuff it back into my bag.

"You always do that, you know?"

"Do what?"

"When you get compliments on your work, you shrug or act all whatever about it, like you don't believe it. Is it just me?"

"No," I say. "It's not just you."

"Then what's going on? Because what's in that book doesn't look like it came from someone who lacks confidence."

Confidence. There's a thing I've always taken for granted. Not that I'm full of myself, but when you grow up with your parents, your teachers, and your friends all telling you how great you are at something, you tend to just believe them. I never really stopped to look at my own work, to try to decide if they were right. And that was why the rejection felt so much like a punch to the chest. It took all the air out of me, and ever since then I've felt like I'm walking around gasping.

"Complicated question?"

I sigh. "You have no idea."

"Oh, but I do," he says, his sigh matching mine. He wanders across the half-grass, half-dust front yard, a cloud kicking up around his boots with each step. He stops at a massive tree stump, sits, and pats a spot next to him. "I'll tell you mine if you tell me yours."

The excuse is on the tip of my tongue. The brush off. But it hangs around for only a fraction of a second before the truth rushes past it with the urgency of a tsunami. I tell him about Governor's School and the paragraph critique that accompanied my rejection. The words that have lived on the page and in my brain feel strange in my mouth, but they still come: "lacks focus and perspective," "underdeveloped," "clichéd." I spit them out like watermelon seeds on hot pavement, and when I'm done I gulp in a breath of the thick summer air. The words taste sour on my tongue, but it feels good to get them out. I never told my parents about the critique. I didn't even show Naz. I just told everyone I got the dreaded "no" letter and shoved the words of the critique through the shredder. But they've been living in the pit of my stomach ever since, like a pesky file I can't delete.

Milo doesn't say anything at first.

"Dee, I'm so sorry. That sounds like a real shit sandwich."

The burst of laughter explodes out of me like a cannonball, and it feels good to release more of the pressure that's built up since that letter arrived. It must have been how he felt when I told him about Pee Pants (again, so sorry Bryce Johnson).

"Can I tell you something?"

"Okay," I say, the laughter calming.

"That critique? That has nothing to do with this," he says. He taps the center of the sketchbook that's balancing on my knees.

"Yeah, but the plan—"

He holds up a hand to silence me. "You've got to quit confusing the plan and the dream. Plans change. They fall apart.

Sometimes outside forces even blow them to smithereens. But the dream is what you always come back to. It's your lighthouse in the fog. In the freaking *storm.*"

I think about that for a minute, my brain catching on the image of my sketchbook on a tiny island, pelted from all directions by rain and wind and waves while a red-and-white-striped lighthouse stands over it, small but sturdy, like the ones I'd seen and sketched on our family's summer trips to Cape Cod. My poor sketchbook is getting beaten and battered, and I want to grab it and hug it to my chest. Like the house, it too feels like an old friend I've been neglecting. I feel the lump rising in my throat, the burn in my eyes telling me the tears are coming. But I don't want to cry. Not about this, and not in front of him.

"It occurs to me that you never told me yours," I say.

Milo lets out a laugh, but there's no joy in it. "Do I even need to? My angry critiques are everywhere. *Milo Ritter has nothing left to say. Milo Ritter needs to find a new career. Milo Ritter is coasting on teen pop stardom.* I honestly can't tell you which hurts worse, the evisceration I got from *Rolling Stone* or the comment below it that simply said, *This album sucks.* That's a pretty damning review right there."

I wonder how I would've reacted if my rejection letter had only said, *This art sucks.* Would it have hurt more, or less? What if it had been public, splashed online for the world to see? The thought makes me feel like my stomach is filled with dirt.

"Well, we're certainly a pair of losers, aren't we?" I say.

"Hey, I wouldn't go that far. We're both Hollywood heavy hitters."

"Uh, you're a heavy hitter. I'm just the bat girl."

"Please, between the canvases you've done for the film and the stuff in this book? It's only a matter of time before you're a bigger deal than I am. So let me be the first to say I knew you when." He reaches out his hand, and I shake it, though what I really want to do is hug him, because somewhere deep in my brain I feel the tiniest flicker of the old flame of confidence that used to burn bright for me.

"I think my parents have you beat on that front. Half the frames on our walls are filled with my work. They're *very* proud parents."

Above us, the sky goes abruptly gray, the cool breeze suddenly feeling less calming and more ominous. The clouds have covered the sun so thoroughly I can hardly believe it was shining just a few minutes ago. I'm pretty sure we're about to get some serious weather. Milo glances up, his hair blowing down into his eyes.

"I think it's time we blow this Popsicle stand," he says. "Let me treat the artist to a meal?"

I smile. "I know just the place. It's not far."

Eleven

Lowell's Roadhouse doesn't have one of those "since 19-blahdy-blah" notations underneath the big orange block letters that are faded nearly beyond recognition, but if I had to guess, I'd say it's at least sometime in the fifties. Dad and I found it on yet another one of our epic wanderings. We'd taken a series of left turns and stumbled upon it just at the moment that we realized we were a) pretty lost, and b) pretty starving. We come back whenever Mom gets heavy into drafting mode and needs total silence in the house. They even let us bring Rubix in, which is good, because he likes to bark at squirrels, which drives Mom batty when she's trying to work.

Milo pulls the truck to a stop next to a row of pickup trucks of various eras, some maybe even original to the restaurant (and with rust to match). I hop out, my sandals hitting the gravel with a satisfying crunch, but Milo pauses to dig a faded blue Dodgers cap out of the center console. He folds the bill in his hands, rounding it out, then pulls it low over his eyes.

"What's with the disguise, Double-Oh-Seven?"

"Just avoiding, you know, uh," he says, swallowing air as he fumbles for an explanation that won't make him sound like a pompous ass.

"What, reporters? Gossip columnists? Paparazzi?" I can barely suppress a laugh imagining someone lurking behind the scraggly boxwoods planted helter-skelter in front of Lowell's, waiting to jump out and snap a photo with a camera as large as the building and probably costing three times as much. "Don't worry. We're out in the county now. No one gives a damn about you. No offense."

"None taken," he says, but he still doesn't remove the cap.

I lead him toward the gray metal door and heave my body against it. Inside, the light is dim and the air is smoky, despite the fact that smoking hasn't been allowed inside Lowell's in a decade. There are only about ten tables in the place, all of which look like they were picked up at a flea market and then thrown off the back of a truck onto a dirt road before being installed in the restaurant. The place is half empty, which is good. Even though I told Milo no one around here gives a damn about a teen megastar, you never know. But a quick scan of the patrons filling the few tables tells me I'm right. It's a scattering of older-looking folks, dirty and tired, like they've been doing manual labor since sunrise. And with the number of working farms and peach orchards around here, they might have.

A waitress in jeans and a tank top, a grease-spattered white apron tied around her waist, is busy dropping beers and picking up empty bottles, while on the tiny stage a middle-aged woman in cowboy boots is doing her best *American Idol* on a cover of "Stand by Your Man." The hand-lettered sign above her head advertises Budweiser and reads "Daily Open Mike, Wednesday Happy Hour." Well, actually, it reads "Daily Open Mik, Wedsday Hap Hr," with the permanent marker falling off the edge of the banner, but I get what they're going for. There's a man at an old wooden upright piano, the kind you see in elementary school music and church choir practice rooms, backing her up, and next to him is an ancient acoustic guitar on a stand. As she finishes her last chorus, the tiny crowd hoots and hollers, making themselves sound twice as large. The woman was good, but it's clear they're more interested in the song than the singer. It's that kind of crowd. Something tells me they wouldn't be down with my usual karaoke choice of "Rapper's Delight."

We take a seat at a picnic table so old and battered that the wood has adopted a sort of soft, oily sheen from years of use and layers of Sharpie where patrons have left their literal mark. Milo reaches for the menus standing in the metal condiment dispenser, wedged between the ketchup and the mustard. He offers one to me, but I shake my head.

"I'm good," I say.

"A regular," he replies.

"Not compared to them." I cock my head toward our fellow diners. "But enough that I know what I like here."

"And that is?" Milo asks. "If there's some kind of local delicacy, I definitely want in. That pimiento cheese at the Diner was amazing."

"I doubt the word 'delicacy' has ever been applied to anything on that menu," I say. I tap my finger on the cloudy plastic cover of the Lowell's menu, which bears pictures of the various items offered from the kitchen. "But if you like Reubens, you won't find a better one."

"Really?"

"Yeah, you doubt it?"

"I just don't tend to associate a good Reuben with Southern dining. Fried chicken? Of course. Something covered in gravy? Definitely. But isn't a Reuben more of an East Coast thing?"

"Snob."

"Guilty."

"Fine, pick something else. Dad says everything is good, and he should know. He's tried it all. But if you're asking me, I'm saying the Reuben."

So when the waitress arrives tableside, pulling a pen out of her ponytail, and Milo orders two Reubens, I can't help the feeling of satisfaction I get.

A few minutes later, after the waitress drops two fizzy Cokes in sweaty plastic cups on our table, we're watching as another singer takes the stage. This time it's a swarthy-looking guy who, if I had to guess, drives long-haul trucks and has a dog named Jack Daniel. He nods at the piano player, who takes his leave, and straps on the acoustic, launching into a peppy version of "On the Road Again." I find myself tapping my toes on the wood floor, silently singing along.

"Do you sing?"

My head snaps back to Milo. "Do I what?"

"Sing," he says. "You know, the moving-your-lips thing you were just doing, but with sound coming out?"

I feel my cheeks flush. "Oh, uh, not really. I mean, shower singing. Car singing. But not, like, *singing*."

"I didn't realize there was such a major distinction."

"Says the professional singer."

Milo throws his hands up. "Hey hey hey, I'm a *musician*. A songwriter on a good day. I'd hardly call myself a singer."

"I didn't realize there was such a major distinction," I shoot back.

"Well, come on. I'm no Frank Sinatra. What people like about me, if they actually like me, isn't my voice."

"Okay. So I'm neither a singer nor a musician, then."

"Yes, I know. You're an *artiste*," he says, twisting the ends of an imaginary Dalí mustache. I stick my tongue out at him, and I get a real laugh in return, one that sends a bolt of energy through me. Seriously, ever since I made Milo laugh the first time in the prop room, it's been like a high I'm chasing. It feels like like it recharges me when my batteries are low.

Our food arrives, the bread bearing grill marks, with yellow bags of off-brand potato chips on the plate next to our sandwiches. I pop my bag and breathe in the salty, greasy smell of the chips, while across the table Milo bites into his sandwich. Sauerkraut and Russian dressing dribble down his chin, along with a string of melted Swiss cheese.

"Good, huh?"

"The best," he says. He swipes at his chin with a napkin from the silver canister on the table. "But don't let anyone from New York hear me say that."

"I doubt anyone from New York has *ever* been in here, so you're safe."

We munch silently for a moment. Overhead I hear the sound of rain picking up, tapping on the tin roof. It's light at first, but soon it's coming down hard enough to drown out the music happening onstage. The trucker has finished up his rendition of "On the Road Again," and is placing the guitar back in the stand. The piano player returns to his post and glances around, but no one moves to take the stage, so he pulls out a crossword puzzle and gets to work.

"I dare you to get up there and sing," Milo says. The request comes out of absolute nowhere, and I can't shake my head furiously enough. "C'mon. I double-dog-dare you."

"Okay, I'm not five. Do you really think that's going to work?"

"I was hoping." He pauses. "Then let's make this interesting. What do you want?"

The question floors me as my brain immediately starts answering it in a million inappropriate ways. As much as I want to follow Naz's advice and be just friends, I can't help my brain from wandering to the darkest corners. What do I want? From Milo? Good Lord. If I keep wandering down that path I'm going to have a hard time thinking of him as a friend. I fear the flaming tomatoes that are my cheeks may be giving me away hard-core. I give my head a slight shake, as if I can erase the damning thoughts like an Etch A Sketch, and quickly try to conjure up something else. Something less, well, blush-inducing. But of course the moment I tell myself *not* to think like that, it's all I can come up with, and suddenly my imaginary make-out session is taking an R-rated turn. I squirm on the picnic bench, then blurt out the first thing that comes to my head that doesn't involve the word "shirtless."

"I'll sing if you do!" I practically bark, and I'm lucky the rain is so loud, or everyone in the joint would be staring at me.

Milo takes another gander around the room, taking in the frayed jeans and faded ball caps, the half-empty beer bottles and the baskets of fries smothered in blankets of ketchup. Then he shrugs.

"Fair enough," he says. For a moment I feel triumphant, until my mind puts together the fact that I just agreed to sing. In front of people. And Milo.

Especially Milo.

Because no matter what he says, the guy can *sing*. His voice is deep and soulful, with just a touch of a growl when he hits the high notes. And yet even with all the character, it's still melodic and somehow beautiful.

But my voice? It's probably something more like Broadway

reject. Junior varsity church choir. I can carry a tune passably, but no one is going to sign me up for a reality show. Not good enough to make it to Hollywood, not bad enough to embarrass myself in the audition rounds, I'd be just one of the many screaming faces in the massive crowd scenes going in and out of commercial breaks.

I never thought he'd agree. He's in deep hiding, after all. But Milo is gesturing toward the stage, and I realize my time has come.

I've only ever sung in public in a karaoke setting, usually with Naz and a big crowd, shouting into the mike. Never have I ever attempted to actually *sing* in public, unless you count my solo during our "I Love Animals" pageant in the third grade. I sang a verse of "Don Gato" while wearing cat ears and a tail, and I was a hit. But I was eight. I could have been burping the alphabet into a microphone, and the audience still would have thought I was cute.

I climb over the bench and trudge toward the stage, trying not to look like I'm en route to the executioner. The piano man sees me coming and puts his crossword puzzle down on the bench. I walk over and ask him if he knows "These Boots Are Made for Walking," a song that has the benefit of being short *and* in a range that won't frighten nearby dogs.

"Sugar, if I didn't know that song I'd be dragged outta here by my *own* boots," he drawls, and nods toward the mike. I reach for it, and after three hard tugs that nearly result in me clocking myself in the forehead with the old, heavy microphone, I've got it in my hand. I'm staring at my sandals, taking slow deep breaths, as the piano bangs out the opening chords. And within seconds, it's time.

"You keep sayin' you've got something for me," I sing, my voice starting out shaky, missing all of Nancy Sinatra's confidence and swagger. I'm rooted to the ground as if my lyrical boots are buried in cement, one hand on my hip, the other clutching the microphone for dear life. But as I raise my eyes to scan the crowd, I can see that I've picked the right song. The dozen or so heads in front of me immediately start bobbing along to the piano, and a hoot rises up from one of the tables in the back. It makes my voice even out, and the little shake I had on the first line disappears. When I get to the chorus, I can see the head bobs turn into almost full-body chair dancing, and a couple patrons are even clapping along. And before I know it, I'm dancing too. I start with a toe tap, then a short, shuffling walk, but by the second chorus I'm strutting across the tiny stage, pointing into the audience and playing to the intimate crowd.

It's not until I get to the bridge that I let myself look at Milo, still at the picnic table in the back corner. He's standing now, his foot up on the bench of the table. He's one of the clappers. And his grin is as wide as the Mississippi, practically shining a spotlight on me down front.

I shimmy and strut and belt the lyrics right up until the very last "One of these days these boots are gonna walk all over you." And when the piano hits the last chord, I take a bow to what amounts to thundering applause from about fifteen diners.

And I. Feel. Awesome.

I take a final bow and replace the mike, then hop off the stage and skip toward the picnic table. Milo is grinning and laughing, but not *at* me, which is good. When I get to the table, he raises his hand for a high five, which I happily give him.

"Damn, girl. You may not think you can sing, but you sure as hell can *perform*."

"This from a man who did a late-night TV performance with a double horn section and fireworks," I reply. "Whatcha got for us today?"

Milo's face breaks into a mischievous grin. He stands and climbs over the picnic table bench, his lanky body unfolding gracefully. He crosses the floor in five long strides, and once onstage he lifts the acoustic, the frayed strap going over his head as he gives the strings a tentative strum to check for proper tuning. He takes a second to adjust a few of the knobs, then steps to the mike.

The opening chords sound familiar, pinging a spot in my brain that tugs for the title. But I can't quite place it. It's not until he opens his mouth, rasping out the opening lyric, that I recognize the tune.

"Fast Girl," his first and biggest hit. Only instead of upbeat synth pop, this acoustic version somehow further emphasizes the, well, *sex* in the song. And I gasp.

I was right. This song *is* dirty!

Milo knows I've got it, and he shoots a wicked grin toward me. When he launches into the chorus, slow and soulful and somehow even *more* sensual, he winks at me.

And that's when something in my chest cracks open, raining sparks all the way down into my toes.

Screw the photographers and the fans and the Internet insanity. I want him. I unabashedly want him, and I don't think I can play it cool anymore.

Milo strums the last chord, and a smattering of applause comes from the audience. Milo's song choice is not the right one for this crowd, that's for sure. But as he places the guitar in its stand and hops off the stage, I realize that maybe the halted applause isn't just for the song. A woman with bleached-blond hair in a messy pile on top of her head two tables away from us leans over to her companion and whispers something, her eyes on Milo.

I'm immediately on alert. And as he weaves through the tables and chairs, I can see that Milo is, too. He ducks his head and pulls his cap a little lower over his eyes, and he's not even to the table before he's pulling out his wallet. When he finally gets here, he deposits way more than two Reubens and two Cokes costs onto the table.

"I'm sorry, but we need to—"

"Yeah, of course," I say, jumping up so fast I bash my knee on the bottom of the table, sending a fork clattering to the floor. *Good one, Dee. So much for a stealthy exit.*

Milo is a step ahead of me, heading toward the door, and I quickly follow. As I pass the last table of diners, I hear someone mutter, "Hey, isn't that that boy-band kid?"

Just before he's out the door, Milo turns, a giddy grin on his face, and calls over his shoulder, "I was never in a boy band!"

And then we're out the door.

The rain is quickly turning the gravel parking lot into a lake, and I feel water pool around my ankles as my sandals slap on the water. The air feels heavy, like I could reach out and part it like a curtain. I swipe the back of my neck where my curls are wet and sticking. A flash of lightning illuminates the sky. Milo starts counting. "One, two—"

He's barely said the words before he's cut off by a rumble of thunder that sounds like it's ready to bowl us right over. It's followed quickly by several more flashes and more rumbles. I can't tell if the ground is *actually* shaking or if I'm just imagining it, but I don't have time to figure it out. The storm is close. The sky opens up further with a loud crack, and the rain pours in big fat drops and wide sheets, coming down more like an amusement-park water feature than an act of nature.

The rain feels good, like it's dissipating the hot air all around me. For a moment all I can hear are rumbles of thunder amid the pouring rain. We run to the truck, Milo's long legs letting him beat me there. He gets to the passenger-side door a few steps before I do and fumbles in his pocket for the keys. I'm breathing hard and so is Milo, so I watch his chest rise and fall in front of my eyes. I'm reminded of the Diner just the other day, when I couldn't believe I was so close to him. Now, it feels like I shouldn't be anywhere else. Without even thinking, I lean into him and feel sparks shoot through my chest at the contact.

Milo looks down at me. "Cold?" he asks, but instead of waiting for an answer, he wraps his arms around me. He doesn't pull me closer, though. Instead he pushes me back just a bit. At first I worry that I've invaded too much of his space. That I've been too forward. He may be single, but it's not like he's available. And even if he was, I'm no Lydia Kane. I've definitely violated the just-friends portion of our unspoken agreement, and my mind immediately starts spinning an excuse that will put things back the way they were. I want him, but above all else I don't want to lose him. I don't want to go back to cold, distant, hate-the-world Milo.

But when he dips down, I know why he needed the space.

All I see are eyelashes as he leans in to kiss me, and instead of shrinking back or being shocked, I rise up on my toes to meet him. We crash together with a force that's almost as shocking as the bolts of lightning happening all around us. I look down and watch Milo's hands grasp my hips, then one travels up my side in a way that would be ticklish and probably make me yelp were I not distracted by the action up north. His palm comes to rest on my cheek, and I lean into it. I feel his guitar-player calluses brush just behind my ear, and I let a sigh escape my lips. We kiss, and suddenly everything melts away with the rain. He's not sad or lonely. I'm not lost or uninspired. We're not worried about art or music or exes or cameras. We're not worried about hiding from anything or anyone. He's just Milo, and I'm just Dee. Together.

When we part for air, our chests are heaving in time with the rain, which seems to be tapping out a perfect rhythm on the roof of the truck. I tilt my head back into the window, look up, and laugh. Milo pulls me back in, and I lean my cheek into his chest like I could crawl in for warmth.

Milo pulls back a little. The rain is still coming down, but neither one of us are paying a bit of attention. At this point we're already soaked, so why bother? "Was that okay?" he asks.

I laugh as raindrops run down my nose and cling to my eyelashes. "Okay? Seriously? That was so much more than—"

Before I can finish, Milo leans in and kisses me again. And this time it's even better.

MOM (voice off camera)

We're home! You still up?

MOM comes into DEE'S room, where she's curled up in bed.

MOM

Did you do anything fun while we were gone?
Or did you just marathon some intense paranormal romance?

DEE

Uh . . . something like that.

Twelve

The wait for Monday morning, when I'll see Milo back on set, feels like an *eternity.* I spend all day Sunday on the porch swing, closing my eyes and imagining I'm back at Lowell's, Milo's arms wrapped around me, his lips on mine. The only thing that pulls me out of my daydream is a text from Naz. It's a picture of her toes, painted the coral color I bought her as a going-away gift, buried in the sand. The blue waves of the Atlantic lap at the shore in the background, and next to her left foot is a physics textbook beneath a biography of Marie Curie.

I text back.

The beach makes even science seem relaxing.

:) Everything ok on the home front? she replies.

My thumbs hover over the tiny keyboard on my screen, pausing for a moment before I reply. I want to tell her everything, but I don't know if I could even convey it all in a text. But that's not even the real problem. The problem is that I don't want to tell her the truth, because part of me is worried she's right. Maybe my heat-seeking missiles are set on self-destruct. Because even though I kissed Milo, and he kissed me back . . . even though we stood on my front porch, just out of reach of the porch light, kissing until I was sure my parents were going to drive up and catch us, even though my stomach is full of a fleet of butterflies . . . there's still the press. And the Internet. And Lydia.

So instead, I type back:

Snooze. Miss you!

I feel instantly guilty about the lie, but I know what Naz would say if I told her. First of all, she'd totally freak out. Then, when she stopped being shocked, she'd lecture me and bring up paparazzi and distractions and all the things that are there, but that Milo's kiss seems to make disappear. And it would all be true, but I don't want anything dialing back my bliss right now. Practical thoughts, the kind Naz specializes in, will only dull the magical memory. And I'm basically living in that memory until I can get back to work.

Finally, *finally* my alarm goes off on Monday morning, and I leap out of bed like I've been ejected from it. I don't think I've ever woken up more ready for a day in my life. Every part of me feels electrified. I don't even freak out about what I'm going to wear. I pick a pair of jeans and one of my favorite broken-in T-shirts from my closet, but I think I'd feel great in a potato sack.

When I arrive at the studio, Milo's truck is in the parking spot where his Audi used to be, and just the sight of it has me biting my bottom lip to suppress the lunatic grin that's threatening to take over my face. It feels like there's an entire army of helicopters buzzing around inside me, and the excited jitters mean it takes me three tries to get my bike locked before I practically skip through the front door. I'm just glad I manage to open it instead of bursting through it like a cartoon.

As soon as I walk in, I can tell that I'm not the only one carrying a load of excitement with me. In the office, phones are ringing off the hook, people are rushing in and out of the room murmuring into their headsets, and the copy machine is spitting out so many sheets of paper I think I just heard it sigh. And in the back, through a window into a small office, I see Rob and Leigh, the executive producer, who I've barely seen since the first day, bent over a binder intently marking pages with pencils. Something is definitely up.

"Ruth needs you. Emergency," Carly says by way of drive-by instructions. She's gone before I can even respond, her zip-up hoodie flapping behind her.

Ruth, it turns out, is having an emergency of the floral persuasion. When I walk into the prop room, I'm greeted with a giant corkboard half full of photos of flowers in every shade and shape, and the work table has been overtaken by an army of vases lined up in neat rows and columns.

"All the flower arrangements for scene eleven need to be reworked. They clash," she says, though she doesn't say with what. She thrusts a stack of photos into my hands. "Get these up on the board so Rob can approve. Toss all the reds. They won't work anymore."

The calm that came over her when we started shooting seems to have temporarily disappeared, and she's back to charging around the prop room, alternately muttering to herself and whoever is on the other end of her walkie-talkie.

When I'm done with the corkboard, Ruth arrives with a bucket of flowers and another stack of photos, telling me to recreate them as best I can with the vases on the table. Flower arrangement has never been a career I've considered, but once I get started it feels fairly familiar. It's all about color and composition, making sure the heights of the various flowers are visually pleasing, that nothing is pulling focus, that there aren't any dead spaces (both literally *and* figuratively, I realize as I toss a half-brown lavender rose into the trash can).

When Ruth calls lunch, my fingers feel raw from where I kept getting the thorns on the long-stemmed roses, and my nose is itchy and runny from the pollen. Turns out floral arrangement is a bit of a contact sport. But Ruth seems happy with my work, or at least I think that's what it means when she nods, her mouth set in a firm line, so I don't complain.

Besides, lunch means I'm finally going to see Milo. Just the thought has my poor, pricked fingers lingering on my lips as once again I let myself relive the kiss in the rain.

When I get to crafty (as I've noticed the rest of the crew calling it), I hop in the buffet line and allow myself a surreptitious glance around. My eyes go to him immediately, like a compass being pulled toward north. He's hunched over a plate, his back to me, already in wardrobe for his next scene. His character's tattoos have been applied to his left bicep and forearm, thick and black against his lightly tanned skin.

"You gonna go?"

While I've been standing here swooning over Milo Ritter's fake tattoos, the buffet line has moved, making it clear to everyone behind me that my brain is somewhere else.

I apologize, then pack my plate full from today's selection of pastas. Everything from marinara to alfredo to puttanesca to some kind of roasted vegetable situation is steaming from the chafing dishes, and I decide to take a tour of Italy and sample them all.

After adding a lump of crispy, buttery garlic bread to my plate, it's time. Because I'm so jittery, I pause to steady myself so I don't have an unfortunate marinara incident on the way over, then I head toward him. I force my pace to be slow and casual, so that when I finally reach him it might actually look like I was heading for the door and stopped to have lunch with him as an afterthought. Set is a closed world, and everyone's discreet. They're contractually obligated to be. But gossip still spreads like a turn-of-the-century epidemic within these four walls, and I don't know what the rules are when it comes to dating the star.

I put my plate down on the table and climb over the bench. Milo looks from the plate to me, a smile breaking across his face, though he quickly dials it back. Clearly he's of the same mind as me, and I'm glad I exercised control instead of beelining straight for him like my legs wanted me to.

"Hey there," he says, and it's a good thing I'm already sitting down, or my legs would give out beneath me.

"Nice lunch," I say. I eye the obscenely healthy collection of vegetables decorating his plate, including a scoop of what is probably lean, fat-free tuna salad in the middle. I make a big show out of swirling a heaping helping of creamy fettuccini alfredo onto my fork, then taking a bite with a loud "Mmmmmm."

"You're evil," Milo says. He stabs at a piece of raw cauliflower and sticks it right in his mouth, no ranch dressing or onion dip or anything. I have to suppress a gag. "Saturday was my cheat day, which I'm allowed since I spend the other six days eating like an Olympic gymnast and bench-pressing my body weight under the watchful eye of a trainer who I think studied at the Fascist Dictator School of Motivation."

He barely gets a forkful of tuna in his mouth before Carly appears behind him.

"Milo, Rob is calling for you in the office," she says, and picks up his plate. "Want me to box this up for you?"

Milo flashes me a smile. "Gotta go. Sorry for the short lunch," he says, nodding at Carly, who disappears in search of a box. I nod and shrug to mask my supreme disappointment that our lunch lasted all of three minutes, partially for his benefit, and partially for Carly, who is back with a white to-go box in hand. But apparently I'm not as good an actor as Milo.

"Making friends, I see?" Carly's left eyebrow rises just enough to let me know that she knows, and that she wants me to *know* that she knows. "When you need a big-sisterly lecture, just say the word. In the meantime, take this to him, 'kay?"

I make my way back into the office part of the building and down the beige-carpeted hallway toward the conference room. Outside the door, I stop and check my shirt again for any stray pasta sauce, then breathe into my cupped hand to be sure I don't have the kind of garlic breath that would clear a room.

Rob is sitting at the head of the conference table in the white, windowless room. To his right is Leigh. Between the two of them, there are four cell phones, a pager, two tablets, and two walkie-talkies resting on the table, along with a clipboard and a stack of papers.

Also at the table are Paul and Gillian, along with a younger blond guy I recognize from that TV show about Chicago police, who I think plays Milo's best friend in the movie but who hasn't been on set yet for any scenes.

When I step into the room, all six heads snap in my direction. Rob and Leigh take one look at me and go back to the array of devices in front of them. When everyone else realizes I'm not who Rob and Leigh were expecting, they go back to chatting or flipping through papers. Only Milo smiles at me.

I hold up the box by way of explanation, and he waves me

over. I squeeze around the edge of the room, sucking in until Gillian Forsyth realizes what I'm doing and scoots her chair in.

"Thank you," I whisper. She smiles at me and tosses her long red hair, the freckles on her cheeks squinching together. It always seemed like she was a nice person when I'd see her on awards shows or in interviews, and I'm glad to see I wasn't wrong.

When I get to Milo, I place the box on the table in front of him and pull the silverware out of my back pocket. "Carly asked me to bring this to you," I say, working hard to keep my voice low.

"Thanks," he replies. He takes the silverware and puts it on top of the box. He glances over at Rob, who's deep in hushed conversation with Leigh. Then he turns back to me. "Looks like we've got our new Kass. She's on her way."

"Who is it?" I ask, then realize too late that this is probably not the time and also probably not my job to ask.

"Dunno," he says. "They haven't said yet."

"'Scuse me, is there tuna in that box?" Paul looks up from the script he's been reading.

"Yeah, man," Milo says. He flips the box open to reveal the scoop of tuna salad on a bed of spinach. Paul recoils.

"I'm sorry, tuna makes me, well, I had a bad experience, so, um . . ." He leans back in his seat and covers his nose with his hand. I can see the color start to drain from his face. Any second he'll be the same color as the wall behind him. Milo notices and quickly closes the box, shoving it into my hands.

"Yeah, totally, no problem," Milo replies, giving me a *yikes* look. I take the box and turn, squeezing past Gillian again. I get to the door and shove it open, noticing that it swings a lot easier than it did when I came in. *That's weird.*

And then all of a sudden the box bursts open, sending tuna salad, spinach, and the serving of pickled beets that were also in there cascading down the front of the tall, thin body that I'm now smashing into.

"OhmyGod!" I shout. I step back, the box falling to the floor between our feet.

"Holy shit!" the girl screeches, shaking her hands hard to release the spinach that's clinging to her fingers. She looks down at the blossoming red stain that's growing on her gauzy white tank top, then looks up at me. She gives her impossibly long red hair a shake to keep it from mingling with the tuna that's clinging to her chest.

"Holy shit," I mutter.

"Holy shit," I hear Milo say behind me.

"I'm going to be sick," says Paul, rushing past us and the whole mess while the blond guy doubles over with laughter. (Aiden! Aiden Lloyd. *That's* his name. Of course it occurrs to me at this moment.)

"Could you get some paper towels?" Rob snaps from his position at the head of the table. He rises from his chair and gestures to an empty one next to Leigh. "We can't have our star covered in someone's lunch. Everybody, I assume you know Lydia Kane."

Thirteen

I don't know what Rob means by *You know Lydia Kane.* I mean, I know Lydia Kane is famous. I know she's got one of those naturally husky voices that makes her sound like she's been carrying on a conversation at a Metallica concert for the past six months. I know she's the kind of person who's frequently photographed in the front row of fashion shows or exiting shiny black cars, sometimes sans underpants.

And I know that her ex-boyfriend is perhaps the best kisser this side of the Mason-Dixon line.

But Lydia Kane and I have never, you know, *been introduced.*

"You, with the food. Get paper towels," Rob says, waving a finger in my direction and then shooing me toward the door. I bend down and retrieve the crumpled, dripping box from the floor.

"And wardrobe, *please,*" Lydia groans, just barely masking the bite in her tone. "I smell like a fish counter."

And then, in front of me and her director and her fellow costars, Lydia Kane peels off her white (and now also red) top to reveal a tanned and taut abdomen and one of those lacy white bras with just enough fabric so as not to be completely see-through. She tosses the tank at me, and it lands in a gauzy heap on top of the crumpled box of dripping food, one of the straps hooked around the plastic ID card attached to my lanyard.

I want to look at Milo to see what his reaction is to this. His ex-girlfriend? Onto whom I just dumped his lunch? Who is now standing in front of him and me and everyone else *with no shirt on*? Of course I want to know. But I also don't, because what if his eyes are on that lacy bra? Or the bit of black scrollwork coming out the top of her *very*-low-rise jeans? I'm pretty sure that, despite my best intentions, I'd burst into tears. Or maybe flames. Either way, it would not be good for him or me or the current state of my employment.

Instead I mutter a few words that I think come out sounding like "I'll go right now," and then dart for the door without a single glance over my shoulder.

I hear the door click shut behind me as I'm dumping the mangled box of food into a trash can at the end of the hall. I toss Lydia's shirt over my shoulder like a hand towel and stop myself from using it as one, opting instead to fling the excess tuna off my fingers into the garbage can and then give my hands a good rubdown on the thighs of my jeans. I guess *I'll* smell like a fish counter all day now.

Carly, who was flying around the corner ready to barrel down the hall, skids to a stop in front of me. Her nose wrinkles as the scent of tuna salad wafts into her nostrils, her eyes running over the streaks of beet juice on my hands and shirt and probably other places I can't think about right now. "Do I even want to know?" she asks.

"No, you don't," I reply. "I need paper towels and wardrobe."

"If you think they're going to loan you a shirt because you couldn't manage to feed yourself, you're high," Carly says.

"Not for me. For Lydia," I say. I see her brow wrinkle, and I realize I'm a step ahead of her. If Milo and the cast are only just now finding out, the crew must still be in the dark. "Lydia Kane."

Carly's eyes go wide, her mouth dropping open a fraction of an inch before clamping shut again. Then I notice her shoulders shaking with poorly suppressed laughter.

"Oh, girl," she says. "I do *not* envy you."

Not *all* the crew members are in the dark, apparently.

I follow Carly's directions to a large room at the back of the main offices that looks like a clothing store's stockroom. Rows and rows of racks fill the space, holding plastic garment bags with large white tags dangling from every piece. There's a long white table in the corner filled with jewelry and other small accessories, and underneath are mountains of shoe boxes with Polaroids taped to the front. The whole room smells like a combination of musty attic and permanent markers.

At the front of the room, two women are working frantically on a half-empty rack that has Lydia Kane's head shot taped to the front of it. Below it is a card with a series of sizes and measurements on it, a bunch of numbers I have to force myself to look away from. I don't know my own measurements, but I'm fairly certain to find them you'd need to add at least five inches to all her numbers except the height, from which you'd subtract . . . well . . . a lot.

A short black woman with a close-cropped pixie and orange reading glasses sliding down her nose glances up at me.

"Extra?" she asks, her tone clipped and urgent.

"Um, actually—" I say.

"Where's your voucher?"

"I don't have a voucher, um, I'm—"

She turns to the girl next to her, who is on her knees next to a box full of shoes, matching up mates and securing them together with giant rubber bands. "Oh, for goodness' sake, how hard is it to give out vouchers? How many times have I told them, *Don't send the extras back here without vouchers*? How many times do I have to send them back before that silly girl gets it?"

The girl with the shoes shakes her head and rolls her eyes as she writes a size number on a manila tag with a very fragrant permanent marker.

"I'm supposed to be—" I try again.

"A pedestrian, yes, yes, we know," the woman says. Her eyes roam over my clothes. "What you're wearing just won't work. Didn't casting tell you not to wear anything with logos? And that shirt has a stain on it"—she gestures to Lydia's top that I have clutched to my chest—"so I don't know why you even brought that. We're not laundresses down here."

"Speak for yourself," the girl on the floor mutters, and blows a wisp of hair that's escaped from her messy bun out of her face.

The brusque woman turns her back to me as she rifles through a rack. She glances over her shoulder at me, her eyes roaming from head to toe. "What are you, an eight? I've got plenty of tops, but no pants for you. You're short, and I don't have time to hem anything. We'll just have to cuff and pin." She whips through the wire hangers so fast they sound like firecrackers popping in quick succession. About midway through she pulls a garment bag from the rack and hands it to me. "Here. You be my dress girl. Eloise will get you some combat boots. Really punky. Change and come back and let me look at you."

Maybe it's the intensity of her expression, or the rabbit hole I feel I've fallen down, or residual shock over seeing Lydia Kane *here* without her shirt on . . . but I silently take the garment bag.

"Go!" she snaps. "If you're not wearing those clothes when I get back you can march your behind back to your car and go home. And you won't get paid for this fitting, either." Then she turns on her heel and disappears down a row of overstuffed racks.

My mouth gapes open and closed like a fish out of water. I want to call out to her, but I don't know her name, and *Hey, wardrobe lady* sounds like something that'll get me slapped.

"Did you need something else?" The girl on the floor with the shoes, who I presume is Eloise, looks up at me, her voice low and her eyes watching the space the woman just vacated.

"Yeah, actually," I say, finally regaining the power of speech. I drop my hand to my side, and the gauzy white tank flutters near the floor like a white flag of surrender. My laminated crew badge catches the light, and Eloise chuckles.

"So you're *not* an extra," she says. She stands and takes the garment bag from me, carefully hanging it in its rightful place back on the rack. She turns to me, a rueful grin on her face. "What did you need?"

I take a deep breath, and start with the tank. "Lydia Kane asked for wardrobe. She was wearing this when, um, she had an unfortunate lunch incident. I'm not sure what you do for—"

Eloise rolls her eyes again, which seems to be her default response to pretty much any situation, then quickly whips around to Lydia's rack. "Was she wearing jeans?" she asks as she leafs through the hangers.

"Yep."

"Black shoes or brown?"

"I didn't see," I reply, thinking I was too busy trying to avert my gaze from her nearly bare chest.

Eloise whips back around, a hanger in hand with a similar gauzy white top on it, this one with delicate straps that tie at the shoulders and a white-to-gray-to-black-ombré dye job at the bottom. "Take this. Should work. And I'll take that." She gestures to the stained shirt. "Because unlike Gloria, I *am* a laundress."

I trade her the dirty top for the clean one and give her my most grateful smile. "Thank you so much," I say. "I'm Dee, by the way."

"Eloise," she says, offering her hand. Her forearm is stacked high with silver bangles that clang when she moves. "Wardrobe assistant. Or more accurately, an assistant to an assistant to an assistant. Or something. I'm like, the lowest on the totem pole around here."

"I know the feeling," I reply. Eloise is the first person to bond with me over my lack of clout, and I appreciate it.

"Sorry about Gloria. She gets grumpy when she has to dress extras, but it's her own fault. She didn't realize when she sent everyone else off to scour the Goodwill that she'd be the one left to do this."

Carly pokes her head into the room.

"Lydia wants to know where her shirt is, as does the rest of the cast," she says. A wad of paper towels crinkles in her hand as she reaches up to adjust her earpiece. "I've got the paper towels, and you'll tell me what the hell happened in there later. Do you want me to take that?"

I pause at the offer. Under any circumstances pre–fifteen minutes ago, I would have said *Hell no.* Any chance to be in a room with Milo is one I'm taking. But now that I know I'll be walking back in to hand a shirt to a topless Lydia Kane while Milo is thinking who knows what in the corner? While I'm wearing jeans and a T-shirt advertising my fifth-grade participation in the Cherry Blossom Festival children's choir and looking like some common . . . *teenager*? Yeah, no thanks.

I hold up the hanger Eloise gave me and offer it to Carly. "Please."

Carly nods, crosses the floor, and takes the hanger, but not before offering me what looks to be a bit of pity. It turns my stomach, because I know I'm oh-so-deserving of it. How have my circumstances catapulted so drastically in such a short period of time? "I'll have that lecture on standby," she says before she leaves.

I turn to Eloise. "Thank you for this. And you'll explain to Gloria?" Which is me asking if I can still get the hell out of here before she gets back, because frankly that lady scares me. And the last thing I need right now is to be chastised on top of pitied.

"Don't worry, she's probably already forgotten," Eloise says. "So long as you're gone before she gets back."

I mouth a silent thank-you and hustle out the door.

I walk through the next hour as if in a dream. I'm so dazed I actually bump into a rack full of glassware, and it wobbles and clinks ominously. Ruth huffs, and I can tell she's about had it with me for today. She thrusts two large ceramic vases into my hands, one tall and skinny, the other short and squat, both a deep-blue color.

"Yup, copy," she says into her headset, then looks at me. "Can you take these to set? And by that I mean, *can* you do it without breaking them?"

I nod, feeling worse by the minute. I've got to pull myself together.

"Good. Rob needs to pick one. You can hang around to bring the other back."

As I make my way down the hall, dodging crew and office PAs running back and forth to set, I give myself a mental pep talk.

Lydia is here. Okay. Milo has done nothing to indicate that he's happy about that. The only reason I don't know for sure is that I bolted before he could reassure me. I'm sure if I had glanced across the conference room, I would have seen the same look of horror and misery that I probably had (and maybe still have). And then he would have pried his eyes away from Lydia and her stupid bra to give me an Oh my God/Can you believe this/I don't want her here/I only want you *look. Which is totally a thing. I mean, if anyone is capable of saying* all that *without saying anything at all, surely it's Milo.*

Right?

The attic set once again looks like a human beehive. Milo is filming in Jonas's apartment, and everyone is bustling around preparing for the first shot of the day. The space is lit both from within and outside, so it looks like sunlight is streaming in through the windows. Rob is standing in the corner near a window, staring at a light meter with one of the lighting guys whose name I don't know. I don't see Milo or the chair with his name on the back anywhere. "Ruth wants to know if any of these work," I say when Rob finally looks up at me.

"Yeah, drop them over on that bureau," he says. He waves a finger toward a hulking antique dresser beneath a window. "I'll pick one and send the rest back later."

I make my way through the cramped space, carefully stepping over the extension cords that are crisscrossing the floor. I gently place the vases on the dresser top, and am turning to leave when a familiar voice catches my attention.

"What are you *doing* here, Lydia?"

I peek out the tiny fake window built into the wall and catch a glimpse of Milo, who's sitting in one of those tall director's chairs, a script on his lap. There's a touch of bitterness in his voice, the anger that he carried around for the first week finally finding its intended target. I don't see Lydia, but she's nearby, because I hear her answer as clear as if she were standing right next to me.

"My job," she says, but she doesn't sound bitchy. In fact, there's a bit of pleading in her voice.

Milo sighs.

"I know you're hurt," Lydia continues. "And mad. And you have every right to be. But you can be those things and still be in love with me."

The words hit me like a ten-ton train right to my chest. I inhale sharply, then flatten myself against the wall of the set so Milo and Lydia won't see me through the prop window. Rob is still engrossed in his light meter and hasn't noticed that I'm skulking around his set, listening in on his actors having some kind of serious emotional conversation.

"Lydia, you didn't forget my birthday or wreck my car. You *cheated on me.* You're acting like it's no big deal," Milo says, his voice razor sharp, like he's talking through clenched teeth. Angry Milo is back with a *vengeance.* I find myself nodding along with him. *Yeah, Lydia. You cheated.*

"It's a huge deal, and the biggest mistake of my life," Lydia replies. Now her voice is soft and impossibly sad. If I didn't know better, I'd feel sorry for her. "I'm going to spend forever trying to make it up to you, because I still love you. And I know you still love me. I can see it all over your face. That's not nothing."

I feel a sour, acidy taste in the back of my throat, and my cheeks burn. In front of me, Rob turns, and I know if he spots me he's going to ask what I'm still doing here. And if I can hear Milo and Lydia, then they can definitely hear me. I feel like I'm going to cry, and I don't want to do that in front of Lydia. Or Milo. Or more than twenty members of the crew, plus an Oscar-winning director. Sure, the crew have perfected the art of keeping their faces impassive, but they're still absorbing every single thing going on around them. If I cry now, I'll be the topic du jour at lunch today and every day. The pathetic PA who fell in love with the star and then cried about it in the middle of set.

I can't be that girl, no matter how much she feels like me right now.

So before I can get outed as a spy, I tiptoe back through the attic set and out the opening at the far end, wishing I could leave what I just heard behind. But it follows me all the way out, nipping at my heels and pinging in my gut.

Fourteen

Every time I closed my eyes last night I saw Lydia Kane standing shirtless in the conference room. "You still love me," dream Lydia murmured over and over. When my alarm goes off at seven a.m., I have no idea how much I actually slept, but it feels like not at all. Which is not good, considering today is our first location shoot.

I pull myself out of the seat of the white van that's ferrying crew members from the studio to Wilder's town square, where we're filming for the morning.

Carly pauses for a moment, glancing through the notes on her ever-present clipboard. "Check with Ruth, and if she doesn't have anything for you, I'll have you with me. There's always lots of random running to be done." She gives me an up-and-down. "And you look pretty spry."

Working on no sleep and an emotional state that has me feeling like I was thrown from a moving car, I feel anything but spry. But I vow not to let any of it show. Not that it appears to be working.

Carly gives me another look and opens her mouth like she's about to lecture me, then snaps it closed again. She sighs.

"I'm here if you need me," she says, then waves me off to find Ruth. It takes a few minutes of wandering between camera rigs and peeking into the backs of the various trucks production has rented to haul in props and wardrobe and equipment. But I eventually find her loading a rolling cart with props for the small group of street-scene extras we have on set today. As soon as I walk up, she hands me a stack of newspapers, all fake unless we've inaugurated a President Jones and I missed it.

"Here, separate these and make them look read, okay?"

Having never actually read a physical newspaper, just the online variety, I'm not sure what that's supposed to look like, but I set about dividing up the sections and giving them a few extra folds and crinkles.

"You guys ready for background?" Benny skips up in what I'm coming to realize is his own personal uniform, this time with yellow knee socks, yellow bandanna, and banana-yellow T-shirt. He looks like a foreman at a banana factory.

"Yep, send 'em over," Ruth replies, and a few minutes later a small group of people hired to be living scenery file past the cart. Ruth gives each of them a quick glance, then shoves props into their hands. "Please remember what you've got, and please make sure you return it to the cart between takes," she barks as she hands a coffee cup and a briefcase to a guy in a suit who's already sweating buckets. As the last of the extras receives a prop, Benny reappears to direct them toward the set.

"Hey, I gotta ask," I say to him. "What's with the outfit?"

Benny cocks his head at me, a blank look on his face. "What do you mean?"

"Seriously?" He's got to be messing with me, but he's actually a really good actor so it's hard to tell.

He laughs. "Okay. Well, it's dumb, but I'm trying to make this crew-color-war thing happen. You get points for your team for dressing up, so see, I've got the PAs three points already."

"How's that going?" I glance around at the rest of the crew, most of whom are wearing jeans and T-shirts commemorating the various films and shows they've worked on.

"It's a slow burn," he replies with a chuckle. "Hey, you wanna join? Wednesday is green day!"

"Green makes me look diseased," I say, "but good luck to you!"

"Just think about it," he replies. "The lighting guys bet me fifty bucks plus some kind of embarrassing task they'll pick later that I couldn't get anyone else on board, and I could really use that money. Help an old friend out?"

I want to hug Benny for making me feel normal again, reminding me of life before the crazy world of film production and kissing celebrities. I feel like I can breathe again.

"If you're willing to talk profit sharing," I say, a smile coming naturally for the first time all morning.

“I’m in for sixty-forty!” he calls as he bounds off after the last of the extras. He turns and mouths a dramatic “please” while folding his hands in mock prayer. I shrug a “we’ll see” in response.

The scene we’re shooting today is simple. Kass, Jonas’s love interest, runs into Jonas outside the bakery where she works. It’s the first time they’ve seen each other since the party where they met (a scene we’re shooting later in the week). It’s only about ten lines, but according to the production schedule, we’ll be shooting it for a couple of hours. Which means I’ll be spending the next few hours on set with Lydia, my first time seeing her since the great shirtless escapade of yesterday.

Because Kass is supposed to be sort of a tomboy, Lydia is in jeans and tennis shoes, a ratty tank top and hoodie on top. She’s dressed like me, actually, only a really good-looking version of me. Her hair is falling down her shoulders in these loose waves that are what Hollywood thinks a normal person’s hair looks like when she’s just walking down the street, the sort of hair that takes a hell of a lot of effort to look that effortless. I know, because a team of hair and makeup people have been following her around like bodyguards, attacking her with picks and combs and hair spray every time there’s a hint of a breeze.

Milo jumps out of a van that’s brought him over from Peach Street, where they’ve parked his and Lydia’s trailers. His fake tattoos poke out from the sleeve of a white T-shirt, and his hair is perfectly mussed. I feel an instant rush of attraction, but it’s tempered by a sense of unease. I have no idea where we stand, but the fact that this is the first time I've seen him since Lydia burst onto the scene (literally) feels like an answer. When he finally notices me behind a camera, he smiles, but it's halting and doesn't quite reach his eyes. I have to look away before my face betrays all the confusion and misery I'm feeling.

Ruth tells me to stay by the cart and make sure the extras drop their props between shots, which means I have a front-row seat to the filming, and I quickly realize why it's going to take so long to get such a short scene. First they have to film it from several angles, including close-ups of both Lydia and Milo. They put a camera inside the bank to get the shot through the window. They spend a couple shots moving extras around, pausing for the extra who sneezed, and the one who got a little too animated about the fake conversation she was meant to be having.

When the camera crew move the equipment to get Lydia's close-up, Benny has the extras step off to the side. Most of them won't get seen in the tight shot, but they need to be close by in case they're needed as blurs in the deep background. They gather next to the prop cart, where I remind them to drop their stuff. Then they turn to watch the train wreck.

Because the thing that makes this whole experience take the longest is the fact that Lydia can't seem to remember her lines. Not a single solitary one.

She's *supposed* to be saying, "I want to help you bust out of this no-good, nothing, nowhere town."

But she can't seem to get past the first half of it before stumbling over the alliteration. By the sixth mistake I have to stop myself from shouting the line myself. The extras are sweating, but they can't fan themselves for fear of making noise that might get picked up by the boom mike. The crew, also roasting, are starting to look annoyed bordering on murderous. I can see a rustle of unease coming from video village, the tent where all the bigwigs are sitting, shielded from the sun, watching the filming on little monitors. When Lydia flubs the line *again,* I see Rob rip off the headphones that are allowing him to hear the dialogue.

Rob mutters something, and then Kathleen, our script supervisor, comes out from the little tent. She's got a black binder tucked under her arm, which I assume has the script inside. From my cheat sheet, I know that a script supervisor is the one who makes sure the actors don't go too far astray from what's written in the script, and if they do, it doesn't take the story in the wrong direction. When she exits the tent, it's never with good news.

"Lydia, I really need you to land this line hard," she says, poking at a spot in the middle of her binder. "It sets up the following two scenes, and if it's too soft, we lose that narrative thread." It's the nicest way Kathleen could probably ask her to *say the damn line*, and I'm impressed with her diplomacy.

Lydia's cheeks redden, because even though Kathleen is being nice, Lydia knows what she really means, as does everyone else on set. But embarrassment doesn't seem to be an emotion that Lydia Kane is comfortable with, so she quickly adjusts to one that's more familiar: anger. She calls Rob out of the tent, where he's working hard to keep his face impassive.

"Can you ask those extras to like, turn around or something?" she says, her voice snapping like a basket of vipers. "They're staring at me, and I can't concentrate."

Rob blinks hard and slow at her, but otherwise his face remains unreadable. He takes a breath, cracks his neck, then turns. "Can we get all the extras to please move over that way?" He gestures with the rolled-up pages in his hand, shooing the extras away like stray pigeons. "And, um, also face that way?"

He drops his sunglasses back down on his face to hide the *Oh my God, am I really doing this?* expression that I'm sure is written all over it. All around me, I see crew members stomping around set moving lights and cables, dragging camera parts and adjusting props, and they're all carefully staring at the ground, trying desperately not to roll their eyes. Benny appears quickly to make sure all the extras are following instructions. He catches my eye and shoots me a quick eye roll. The solidarity of Lydia Kane being the worst is comforting. I return the eye roll, combining it with an exasperated head shake.

I let myself consider it a victory. Milo is seeing all this. He can't like it, surely. He's going to have a hard time forgiving her cheating if she's stomping around acting like an A-list diva. At least, that's what I tell myself until my eyes find him on set. Milo is leaning in, whispering in Lydia's ear. Her voluminous hair is blocking his face, but when he steps back I see him give her a small smile. He squeezes her upper arm, and she leans into him ever so slightly.

As soon as the camera has been adjusted for coverage, Rob calls, "Okay, let's go again!" Everyone stops where they are to avoid making any noise that might get picked up on the boom mike. And this time, with the extras facing the opposite direction, Lydia parrots the line just as Kathleen told her to. *Finally.*

We break for lunch just as the sun is highest in the sky. Everyone on set is fanning themselves with whatever stray piece of paper they can find, and those without have rivers of sweat flowing down their backs and across their foreheads. We load onto a van and are driven a few blocks over to an empty storefront that houses craft services for the day. The extras go around to the back to where their food is waiting while I hop in line behind Trevor, the boom mike guy, with the rest of the crew.

"Don't you love it when they live up to their stereotypes?" Trevor says to a camera PA in front of him.

"Did you see Milo huffing around the studio yesterday? He looked like he wanted to set the place on fire," she replies, her voice low as her eyes dart around to make sure she won't be overheard. *Too late.*

"I hope he gets a union stunt double before he attempts it," Trevor says.

I'm glad to hear that Lydia's arrival drove Milo bats, but it doesn't make the weight in the pit of my stomach disappear. I try to ignore it (or possibly drown it) by focusing on the buffet.

I load my plate with another scoop of pulled pork before sliding on down to the salad bar.

I take my food outside and cross the street to the small plot of grass that makes up Wilder's town square. I park under a tree, my bum on top of a root, and balance my plate on my knee.

My sandwich smells amazing, and I'm just about to bite in when something else invades my nostrils. Something sour and sulfury and just generally gross.

Cigarette smoke.

Someone on the other side of this tree has just lit a cigarette, and it's totally ruining my lunch. I don't know why *anyone* smokes nowadays. I mean, it makes you smell like an ashtray and, you know, *kills you.* The hardest thing about being on set is the sheer number of cast and crew who are completely addicted. Smoke breaks seem to be just as important as lunch breaks around here. When I asked Carly about it, she muttered something about how smoking was a thing actors could do that kept them from attacking craft services.

I fan my hand in front of my face to try to send the smell away, but it doesn't help. I try the exaggerated coughing in hopes that whoever has just lit up will take the hint and wander away, but the smoke remains. Finally I lean around the side of the tree to see who it is. From my perch on the ground, the first thing I notice is a pair of black spike-heeled booties, then skinny jeans and legs for miles. My eyes make their way up to the dark-red mermaid hair of Lydia Kane, a cigarette between her fingers. Why she's not in her wardrobe anymore I have no idea, but her new outfit scares the hell out of me.

I'm not about to say boo to Lydia Kane about her smoking, so instead I try to quietly stand and skulk away to a smoke-free lunch spot. But I barely get two steps away before my foot catches on another tree root. I start to fall, but fling an arm out toward the tree trunk to catch myself. I manage to keep myself upright but my plate does not follow me, and my attempts to catch it before it hits the ground send it flying into my left thigh, barbecue sauce soaking into my shorts.

"Are you *kidding me*?" I mutter. Behind me I hear a snort.

"You really need to get that whole walking-while-holding-things situation under control," Lydia says, her voice somehow venomous and bored at the same time.

"Uh, yeah," I reply, clutching my plate to myself to keep more food from spilling. I tilt it and scrape the rest of the contents from my clothes back onto the plate. "I was just leaving."

"I know who you are," she says, taking a long, sultry drag on her cigarette. The smoke escapes out the side of her ruby-red lips.

I gulp and actually think for a moment, *Who am I?* "Oh?" is what I finally settle on for a reply.

She gives me a soap opera–worthy stare, one eyebrow arched so sharply it looks like it could cut into her forehead. "You don't look like someone who's into the cameras and the gossip and all that. It seems all fun and games, but trust me, it's brutal. You'll never survive it."

She drops her cigarette into the dirt and stubs it out with the toe of one of her leather heels. Then she tosses her hair over her shoulder and saunters back across the street toward craft services, leaving me to do nothing but stare, mouth agape, potato salad congealing on my shoe in the sun.

The heat and the cigarette smoke and the smell of hot mayonnaise makes me feel like I'm going to hurl behind this tree. I need a friend. And *fast.* I consider calling Naz and confessing everything. Even one of her lectures would comfort me right now. But she's probably in class or the library.

I hustle back to our temporary cafeteria and find Carly tossing her lunch into one of the giant trash cans.

"I need that big-sister pep talk or whatever," I say. My voice sounds shockingly small, but at least I manage to keep the tears that are itching behind my eyes at bay.

Carly raises an eyebrow at me, then reaches down and switches off her walkie-talkie. "It was actually more of a lecture," she says.

"Whatever, I need it."

Carly takes a seat on one of the gnarled tree roots creeping out of the ground. I plop down in the dirt in front of her.

"I don't know what's going on with you two, and frankly I don't want to know. I'm pretty sure I could guess anyway. One minute you're a walking Valentine's Day card, the next you look like a wilted funeral wreath."

The description makes me laugh in spite of myself, and it comes out a little more sob-sounding than I meant.

Carly's eyes soften, and she sighs. "Lydia is a dragon lady. No one likes her. I don't think even *she* likes her. Anyone with half a brain and two eyes would pick you in a heartbeat. He's screwed up right now, but I'm sure it'll work itself out. Until it does, just focus on work. Okay?"

"That wasn't much of a lecture," I say through a sniffle, though there's a half smile that I can't contain. I never thought Carly, with her clipboard and her rapid pace and her exasperation, would be one for sentiment.

"Midshoot rewrite. The script called for something else," she says. She rises from her perch on the tree root and offers me a hand. I take it, and she hauls me to my feet. She reaches down and flips her walkie-talkie back on, and in an instant she's babbling away into her headset.

The show must go on.

CARLY

~~Falling in love with Milo Ritter is maybe the stupidest thing you could possibly do.~~

CASTING NOTICE

Party Guests

Seeking men and women ages 18–70, all ethnicities, for a cocktail party scene. Upscale look. Must have own cocktail attire. Work Wednesday, June 23. $80/8 hours, plus overtime.

HOW TO APPLY

Email 3 pictures (one above the shoulders, one above the waist, and one full-body) along with your height, weight, age, and phone number to colorextras@vimail.net

Subject: PARTY

Fifteen

I sleep only slightly better than the night before. My alarm buzzes at the criminally early hour of five a.m. for our five-thirty crew call. I don't remember the last time I saw sunrise. I make it a point never to sign up for anything that requires me getting out of bed before seven in the morning. This is part of the reason why I never played sports (the other part being that I have the hand-eye coordination of a drunk toddler).

Today we're on location again, this time for a really big crowd scene that's supposed to take place at a fancy party. Production has taken over the Charlesmark House, a historic antebellum mansion right in the middle of town. The whole cast is in the scene, along with a cavalcade of extras in fancy clothes. It's going to be an all-hands-on-deck kind of day.

I dress in a flash in cutoff denim, one of my dad's old Harvard T-shirts, and a pair of work boots. The forecast calls for temperatures in the upper nineties today, and with late-June humidity, it's going to be a real scorcher. I'd wear flip-flops if that kind of thing were allowed on set (which, I learned recently, definitely is *not,* with all the heavy equipment and rigging, not to mention all the actors and extras stomping around in spike heels).

I pull my car into the Motor Inn parking lot that's serving as base camp for today. There's already a tent set up in the far corner of the lot where extras are milling about, some still in street clothes carrying garment bags, others already dressed for our scene in jewel-toned satin sheaths and crisp black suits. Most of them have big travel mugs of coffee in hand, and a few are already smoking early-morning cigarettes, whatever they can do to wake up. I open the door of the Honda just as the crew van pulls up. Rodney, our driver, rolls down the window.

"You coming to set?" he calls.

"Yep." I grab my bag off the passenger seat and climb into the van, sitting on the first bench seat next to Carly. Eloise, Gloria, and Rob are in the van as well, all talking into their respective phones with the seriousness required to launch a NASA mission. I spot a flash of green in the back row and crane my neck to see Benny, half asleep, leaning against the window, wearing his uniform of cargo shorts, a green T-shirt, and a green bandanna tied around his head. I can't see his feet, but if I had to guess, I'd say he's got matching green knee socks on. As the van shudders to a start, he cracks his eyes open, takes one look at me in Dad's Harvard shirt, mutters "Traitor," and falls back to sleep.

Carly rolls her eyes. "God, I hate days like this," she says. "Fingers crossed it doesn't turn into an unholy disaster."

"What's wrong with days like this?" I ask.

"Are you kidding? Location shoots are hard enough, but when you add in over a hundred extras it's enough to make you wish you'd listened to your mother and become a middle school teacher. At least middle schoolers have some sense of boundaries and propriety. Extras are *the worst.* Capital *T*, capital *W*."

I shrug. They're just background. Glorified scenery, really. Sure, sometimes they sneeze or accidentally look into the camera, but really, how bad can they be? Carly sees my doubt and shakes her head.

"Just a word to the wise? Don't feed the animals."

I don't even know what that means, and I kind of don't want to know. Instead I watch the passing scenery of my town through the van windows as we make our way to the Charlesmark.

The van turns down the circular drive and pulls to a stop in front of the main steps up to the Charlesmark's hulking front door. The house was built in 1859 by Rutherford J. Charles, our town's richest resident at the time. He had a massive plantation, along with all that entails in the pre–Civil War South. I've taken the tour about six or seven times since I moved here, including two visits as part of school field trips.

The place really is a beauty, thanks to Wilder's restoration efforts, and I imagine it'll make a perfect backdrop for a scene in which Jonas, our main character, attends a ritzy party and meets Kass. The whole thing culminates with Kass's mother (played by Gillian) calling Jonas trash.

I climb out of the van, Carly right on my heels.

"I talked to Ruth. She's got a fleet of PAs working props today, so you're with me," she says. "Adrian has point on the extras, but we're all going to need to help corral them." Another animal metaphor. Man, extras get no respect.

We head into the Charlesmark, dodging crew members carting camera pieces up the stairs and through the front door. Despite my many visits to the historic home, today it looks nothing like I remember. The original heart-pine floors are crisscrossed with heavy electrical cables as the lighting guys work on their setup. Mats have been laid down all over the place to protect the parquet flooring from the thumping of work boots and rolling of equipment. There are pieces of neon gaffer's tape marking Xs all over the place, noting marks for the actors in the first scene, and props is crawling all over the set, placing half-empty champagne glasses and plates of hors d'oeuvres on every surface and setting up various fake buffet tables amid all the period antiques. Seeing the heaping tables of cheese, french bread, fruit, and various pastries makes my stomach rumble, even if that food is going to sit out all day and inevitably look seriously wilted by the end of filming.

We make our way straight through the house and out the

back door, where a tent's been set up on the expansive back lawn. A school bus has pulled up alongside it, and extras in their party finery are filing off. The men have their coats draped over their arms, while the women hold the trains of their dresses in one hand, their shoes in the other.

"Ugh," Carly groans, then calls out, "All right, guys, off the bus and into the tent! We'd like to get things started as quickly as possible, so please save your morning cigarettes!"

The extras who've already lit up stub them out and flick them into the grass.

"Excuse me, could we please try to avoid setting the one-hundred-fifty-year-old house on fire?" Carly snaps, waving a finger at them. "We have a bucket over there for your butts. Use it, or we'll send you home."

She turns to me and makes like she's bashing her brains out with her clipboard. "Oy with this day already," she mutters. She nods her head toward the tent. "Can you go in there and back Adrian up?"

If I'm going to take Carly's advice and focus on work, then I need to stay as far away from Lydia as possible. And if there's anywhere Lydia's *not*, it's in extras holding. I wander into the tent, which is crammed full of people and rickety plastic folding chairs. The extras are already congregating, moving the chairs around, fighting over the few power strips that have been set up so they can charge their phones. There's a group of middle-aged extras clutching enormous travel mugs, looking like they've been through this more than once. In the corner is a group of girls who keep giggling nervously and touching up their lipstick, looking like they can't wait to get in front of the camera. A few people have already parked in chairs and nodded off. There are garment bags flung over the back of nearly every chair, and several of the women are perched on the ground using the chairs as vanities while they touch up hair and makeup.

Adrian hustles through the tent flap and climbs up onto one of the chairs. Despite the heat, she's in jeans and boots, a red bandanna tied around her neck like a bandit. Her headset pushes the spiked ends of her black pixie cut in all directions. She's barely five feet, but she has the personality of someone twice that tall. She adjusts her headset so she can cup her hands around her mouth like a megaphone, then calls out for everyone to "shut the hell up.

"All right, guys, there's a lot of you, so I'm going to really need you to listen when someone in a headset is talking," she says once the crowd is quiet. "And if you can't do that, I have no problem sending you home. Just like always, no phones on set. No pictures outside of this tent. No social media-ing about *anything* that happens on set, unless you want to go home and also write a very big check to Rialto Productions. If you're going to smoke, please do it at least ten feet away from the tent, and butts go in the buckets."

After a few more instructions about bathroom locations and not touching anything and three more reminders not to take any pictures—"I mean it," she says with an evil eye combined with the ever-present threat of being sent home—Gloria, Eloise, and a gaggle of other wardrobe folks file into the tent and start wandering through the crowd adjusting straps and ties. A *lot* of double-stick tape gets applied. Gloria lasts about four and a half minutes before she huffs, waves at the wardrobe assistants, and bolts toward the house. Eloise ends up in charge in the tent.

"Excuse me, are we going to get hair and makeup?" asks a girl in a hot-pink satin-and-sequin number who looks like she's already wearing an entire Sephora on her face. Adrian rolls her eyes in response, then turns to me.

"They seriously think that with a hundred and fifty of them, we're going to waste time spackling them up? Fat chance. Most of them won't even get seen."

It turns out getting this show started "as soon as possible" means it's two hours before we even start moving extras into the house for the first scene, which requires about a third of them to dance in the background to silent music while the cast has a quick exchange in the foreground.

Adrian is instructing the extras on how to dance and to definitely *not* look into the camera or at the actors when Carly brings one more group in to join them. Trevor is moving through the crowd with a roll of sticky foam strips, applying them to the bottoms of high heels to prevent the inevitable clacking during the dancing. I've been put on cell phone patrol, making sure no one has brought one onto set.

My own phone vibrates in my back pocket. I whip it out to

see a text from Naz. I haven't heard from her since the beach photo, which is partly my fault. Once I made the decision not to tell her about Milo, I felt guilty sending her anything else. A lie of omission feels slightly better than a slew of outright lies, which is what anything I'd send her at this point would be.

I swipe at the screen, and the message pops up.

IS THIS YOU???

Below the text is a link. Without even clicking on it, the bottom of my stomach drops out. I try to calm myself. When I finally click on the link, service is so slow it takes a moment for the page to load. And once it does, I immediately want to hop the next van back to my house, crawl under my covers, and never come out again.

The picture is small and grainy, and looking again, I have to blink a few times. It's like one of those magic eye puzzles where you have to relax your eyes to get the image, but once you do, it won't go away. The parking lot. The big black truck. Me on my tiptoes, my hand against Milo's chest, while he stoops, his lips pressed to mine.

"Holy shit, is that you?" Carly is by my side, peering over my shoulder.

My silence is answer enough, apparently. Because the grainy cell phone photo is most definitely me. Not that it looks like me at all. I can't believe Carly was even able to come to that conclusion. I can only tell it's me because, well, I was there. And though the memory of the kiss gives me the usual sizzle, it quickly fizzles as the reality of my situation sinks in.

Apparently one of those old-timers at Lowell's knew *exactly* who Milo was.

I scan the page, my finger flicking up and down on the screen, but I'm not identified by name. *Thank God.*

"They don't know it's me," I say, my voice barely above a whisper.

Another text from Naz pings onto the screen.

Normally I'd tell you not to,
because it's the #1 rule of the Internet,
but read the comments . . .

I navigate back and take a deep breath, then click on a hot-pink link below the picture that reads "Comments." I gulp. *Dear God.*

Four hundred and ninety-three bits of text appear. I don't even have to read them to tell that they're full of snark. Between the questionable capitalizations, the strings of emoticons, and oceans of exclamation points, it's sort of hard to miss. Some aimed at Milo, some aimed at Lydia, and quite a bit aimed at me. But that's not what I really focus on. Nope, I can't care about the words "slut," "skank," "rebound," or "nobody," because the "Top Comment," noted with a yellow star and about sixty bajillion likes, simply reads DEANNA WILKIE. Below that is a link to my SocialSquare page (which, thank God, is still private), as well as an article about a community art show I did sophomore year (that's accompanied by a *really* unflattering photo of me holding a blue ribbon . . . let's just say face-framing layers are *not* my best look).

"Look, I know you're having, like, a massive existential breakdown right now, but if you don't put that phone away Rob is going to fully lose his shit," Carly says, glancing around to see if Rob is about to leap out from behind one of the many potted ferns that props has brought in to add some more color and texture to the space. "But we are *so* going to talk about this later."

Oh, we are so *not.*

"Okay, go for rehearsal!" Rob calls. Music kicks on through the speakers placed behind the ferns, and the extras begin dancing. Then, just as abruptly as it began, the music cuts out. But the extras continue as if it were still playing. Lydia enters in a blood-red, gravity-defying strapless dress, a giant white magnolia behind her ear holding back a cascade of cinnamon-colored waves, but she doesn't get a line out before Rob calls cut. "Hey, uh, PA girl? You're in the shot."

I feel the sting of a minimum of fifty pairs of eyes on me. My cheeks burn with the heat of the embarrassment I feel when I realize that yes, I'm standing right in front of the camera while all around me, people in formal wear are fake-dancing to silent music. I glance up to see Lydia shoot me a withering look before turning on one of her impossibly high heels and stomping back to her starting mark at the top of the stairs. And as my eye follows her, Milo appears from around a corner wearing an immaculately tailored black tuxedo. He doesn't notice me standing below in a sea of extras, but I see him. I see him looking devastatingly handsome, and I see him reach over and grab Lydia's hand. He laughs, and then she laughs, and I swear there are literal bolts of electricity zapping back and forth between them.

I bolt from the parlor muttering apologies to anyone who catches my eye. Having visited the Charlesmark House so many times, I know that if I make my way through the atrium and into the kitchen, I'll find a small wooden door painted bright red that will lead me down a flight of stairs into the servants' quarters, which is what Southerners call the slaves quarters so they don't have to think about slavery. I doubt they've got anything set up down there for filming, and sure enough, when I arrive, I find it blissfully empty. Which means I can park myself on the stone floor of the basement, pull out my phone, and further twist the knife by scrolling through the comments.

There's a lot of hand-wringing and sobbing emojis from girls who were hoping Milo would stay with Lydia, or better yet, date *them*. One girl refers to me as a skunk, but I assume she was going for "skank." I keep telling myself I should stop, but just like picking a scab, I can't quit until I'm bleeding. I keep scrolling, keep reading, and with each comment on my hair or my outfit or my face, the pit in my stomach grows.

If they know who I am, it's only a matter of time before there are more photos, these taken with sharper lenses wielded by professional hands. I'll end up on more websites, and maybe even in magazines. I could end up on freaking *TV*.

I think back to Lydia's words the other day, about how I'd get tired of all this. About how I wouldn't last. And I'm starting to understand how she could be right. This sucks. It sucks bad.

I can't watch Milo and Lydia filming today. I can't watch them have their meet-cute or whatever and start falling in love on-screen, because I don't know if I'll be able to separate that from real life. Or if it even *is* separate from real life. So I tell Adrian that I'd be happy to man the extras tent for her. She looks at me like I've just offered her a kidney, and then actually hugs me. She sends me over to get a walkie-talkie and headset and tells me she'll call for me on channel two when she needs me to send extras to set.

"Just keep them quiet and contained, okay?"

It sounded like an easy-enough assignment, maybe even my easiest since I started work on the film. But it turns out that keeping extras contained is like herding kindergartners who are hopped up on Pixy Stix and Mountain Dew. They keep wandering out of the tent to smoke or sneak onto set to get in more shots. While they have their own craft services table in the tent (okay, so it's only a giant tray of Chex Mix and a big orange jug of water), several of them try to sneak out to the back of the property to hit up the crew table. I don't blame them. Today is burrito day, and the smell of cilantro and marinated chicken is enough to make your mouth water, but I quickly learn that nothing sends a crew member over the edge faster than having to stand in line behind an extra to get a bite, especially when they have only a precious few minutes between shots.

Inside the tent is no better. I keep getting approached by extras, all asking in new and different and not-so-subtle ways if they can go to set soon. Several of them try to pump me for contacts, not knowing that I'm an intern with none to speak of. I can't help any of them get famous, which seems to be why most of them are here.

Ultimately I grab one of the folding chairs and take up post outside the tent so I can watch the comings and goings, and hopefully catch them before they make their way to the burrito bar. The rest of the time I spend alternately staring at my rapidly growing in-box and shoving my phone into my pocket, telling myself to stop—*no, really this time, stop!*—obsessing over the photo.

Production has set up sawhorses around the perimeter of the property, which seemed weird to me until, over the course of the day, people began showing up on the sidewalk. Some just peer around, hoping for a sighting of a celebrity; others have phones and cameras and are busy snapping photos. It's not a big deal—there's really nothing to see outside save for the stacks of equipment the lighting crew are storing on the front lawn. Someone may have gotten a truly impressive shot of Steve's butt crack as he hauled a giant stand up the front steps. But otherwise, not much going on.

But there's a flash of something jewel-toned and satiny over by the crowd that catches my attention. I stand up and shield my eyes from the beating sun to try to get a better view. *Has someone from the cast gone down to sign autographs? Oh, that's really nice.*

Only I don't recognize the brunette who's down there, pen in hand, posing for pictures. She's not in the cast, at least not that I know of.

"Who the hell is that?" Benny asks, appearing at my side.

"I don't know," I reply. And then I get a flash of recognition. I saw her getting off the school bus this morning. She's the girl who asked if the extras would be getting hair and makeup, and I'm pretty sure she's asked me to get on set six or seven times. "Holy crap, she's an *extra*."

Benny laughs. "You've got to be kidding me," he says. "Adrian is going to flip her shit when she sees that."

I'm not normally a very confrontational person, and a few hours ago I probably would have jumped at the chance to let Adrian be the bad guy. I might have even enjoyed watching the show. But right now? When I'm taking virtual hits from every Milo Ritter fan in the Western Hemisphere while Lydia Kane's warning haunts my brain? Yeah, I'll take this one.

I snatch the clipboard out of Benny's hand, because I figure I need something to lend me an air of authority, and then march across the lawn. "Hey, you!" I shout. The extra whips around, and her photo-ready smile vanishes. "What in the hell are you doing?"

"I, uh, I w-was just— " she stammers.

"Get the hell back to the extras tent before I send you home," I snap, gesturing toward her path. "Extras *do not* leave the tent. Can you not follow even the simplest of instructions?"

"You mean you're not an actress?" a middle-aged woman in an electric-blue visor drawls as she drops her camera back into her fanny pack.

"I *am* an actress," the girl replies, "just not— "

"Go!" I cut her off, and then, like my mom used to do when I was little, I start counting. I have no idea how high I'm willing to go, or what the consequences will be when I get there, but it doesn't matter because she scurries back up the path toward the tent before I hit three.

I let out a huffy breath and tuck the clipboard under my arm before stomping up behind her. When I get back, Benny is giving me a slow clap while a smile spreads across his face. "Nice one," he says. "Color me impressed."

"Yeah, I had a little frustration to get out," I reply.

"Well, I'd better get back. I'm on camera patrol," he says, rolling his neck and bouncing on his heels a bit. While I've had my chair out here, Benny's been on his feet in the house all day. He's got to be feeling it.

"Camera patrol?" I ask.

"Making sure none of the extras are staring at the camera," he says. "By the way, tomorrow is red. Don't let me down, Wilkie."

I give him a two-fingered salute, then watch as he bounds off toward the house.

I spend the rest of the day on my perch outside the tent. My job is 90 percent pointing out where the bathrooms are, but each time they set up for a new shot inside the mansion, I get to pull a selection of extras to send up to set. I actually find myself having fun pulling out a good mix of people and complementary dress colors from the group, trying to imagine what the camera will see when it pans over the crowd. Adrian even comes down to tell me that Rob is really happy with the way the scene is looking today. "It's crazy unusual for the director to compliment the background," she says, and gives me a good hard slap on the back that nearly knocks the wind out of me.

Soon the sun is starting to set, and on the radio I hear that there's only one more shot before we wrap for the day. Adrian takes up a post at a table inside the tent to start wrapping the extras, meaning signing their pay vouchers and sending them home. We need to retain only a small group to finish up inside, so I stand at the entrance to the tent and make sure everyone's voucher is signed before they leave.

"Voucher?" I ask as they file by, barely registering their faces. They nod or wave their signed slips, but most ignore me. I don't care. Between the early wake-up, hanging around in the sun all day, and fretting about the photo, I'm exhausted. "Voucher? Voucher?"

"Yeah, where do I get that signed again?"

"Ugh, at the table in the tent," I groan, and notice how much I sound like Carly. When I glance up, Milo is standing in front of me in his tuxedo, looking just as sexy as I imagined he would. "Oh, hey," I say, trying to sound cool and breezy and relaxed. Unfortunately, I think I come off sounding strangled.

Milo clears his throat and adopts some sort of weird, professional tone of voice. "Uh, can I talk to you? About tomorrow's scene?" He nods toward the back of the property, away from the prying eyes and iPhones of the tentful of extras.

"Yeah, of course," I reply, trying to match his all-business tone. I follow him across the lawn and around the side of the house, where we're alone and out of sight.

"How's it going?" he asks, but there's a hesitancy in his eyes that tells me he probably already knows.

I take a breath to ensure I won't burst out into sobs. "Well, I'm wrangling a hundred and fifty extras who all think their Oscar-winning close-up is coming any second, I have a blister on my left pinkie toe, and oh, what was that? Yeah, strangers are discussing my love life on the Internet."

He grimaces like he's just witnessed a horrific car crash. And I feel like I've just been through one. "So you saw it, huh?"

"The whole *world* saw it, Milo. I think I was the last one, in fact."

He throws an arm around me and pulls me close. I take a deep breath, but he smells more like the costume closet and the makeup chair than Milo, so it doesn't have the calming effect I was hoping for. "Are you doing okay?"

"Um, I don't know. I mean, you'd think you'd get used to reading grammatically incorrect and questionably capitalized diatribes about your maximum sluttitude, but you'd be wrong."

"I'm really sorry, Dee. I promise, this will blow over. Someone else will crash his car or go to rehab or kiss someone or grocery shop and we'll be yesterday's news."

"Yeah, but until then we're the news *today*, and I don't know how to deal with it," I say, my words muffled by the thick fabric of his jacket. I still can't smell *him*, so I rear back. "Milo, I have six hundred and thirty-one unread emails! And not a single one is from the Gap! That's seriously more emails than I've received in my entire life *combined*. I'm pretty sure my third-grade teacher emailed me—*that's* what my in-box looks like right now."

Nevermind that you're smiling at Lydia and squeezing her arm and the two of you are practically bursting with chemistry. But keep that one to myself. I can't go there yet.

Milo looks pained. "I'm really sorry, Dee. Truly. I really hoped this wouldn't happen. It's what I was trying to avoid," he says. "Listen, I've got to stay tonight for a few more shots, but are we okay?"

I'm not. I'm categorically *not okay*. And I know it, but Milo is so good at convincing me it's all *going to be* okay that I find myself nodding, like maybe if I bob my head enough my boyfriend's ex-girlfriend won't be trying to get him back, and he won't maybe still be in love with her, and a rabid pack of fangirls (and more than a few fanboys) won't be verbally destroying me on the Internet.

"Great," he says. He leans in and plants a soft kiss on my lips. "Maybe we can hang out tomorrow after we wrap for the day? Grab a bite?"

For the first time, a kiss from Milo isn't an instant, blissful fix. There's more than a hint of doubt and defeat that I just can't ignore. But I try, because it's Milo.

"Absolutely," I reply. "Can't wait."

Sixteen

Today is a new day. Today, someone else in Hollywood will get caught making out in a parking lot. Or maybe someone else will punch a paparazzo or start his or her morning with a gallon of tequila or simply take a trip to the grocery store, and Milo and I will be old news. Yesterday's news. *No news.* At least, that's the pep talk I gave myself over and over until I fell asleep last night.

But until that happens, I plan to do all I can to make today better than yesterday and brush off the misery of that website. I want to pretend everything's okay. I want to have *fun*, like I would with Naz (if I hadn't spent my summer lying to her). So when I head to my closet to get dressed for work, I pull out a pair of khaki cargo capris that I haven't worn since middle school and top them with a red tank top. It takes some digging, but I'm able to find an old pair of red knee socks that have white stripes at the knee, left over from a Halloween costume the year Naz and I dressed as ketchup and mustard.

"Hey, Dad!" I call, half in my closet as I riffle through piles for my other shoe.

"You bellowed?" Dad pokes his head in my room, already dressed for his morning run.

"Yeah, you have a red bandanna, right?"

Dad takes a glance at my outfit. "Did you join some kind of gang?"

"Yes. Yes, I did," I reply, gesturing to my knee socks and matching tank top. "I've joined up with some local street toughs. This is our uniform. This evening we plan to knock over the local soda fountain and then lean against some light posts while we comb our hair and whistle show tunes."

"Smart mouth," he says, shaking his head at me. "I taught you well."

"Bandanna?"

"Top drawer of my dresser!" he calls as he heads down the hall, already bouncing on the balls of his feet. He'll be halfway down the block before I even finish tying my shoes. I've tried to explain to him that he's doing summer vacation exactly wrong. You don't get up early and exercise. You binge-watch police procedurals and reality shows about rich women without jobs while seeing how many different varieties of potato chip you can consume in one sitting without throwing up. But he insists on the whole running thing, so I've given up.

I find the bandanna and tie it around my head after

gathering my pouf of curls into twin pigtails. I take a glance in the full-length mirror mounted on the back of my parents' bedroom door. I look a little like a 1970s gym coach. I hope Benny appreciates what a good friend I am. And I hope the outfit masks the doubt that's practically rattling in my bones.

The sun is only just starting to peek over the trees, so the air outside is still slightly cool and very damp. The road has a haze across it as I scream down the back country roads to the gristmill.

Dad's Honda bounces down the dirt-road entrance, kicking up a cloud of red Georgia clay behind it. I follow the yellow direction signs that I've come to know well to the grassy clearing marked CREW PARKING. I pull up and stop at the end of a row of cars, park, and climb out to catch the van the rest of the way to the Thorpe Creek Gristmill, the location for today's shoot.

The mill is ancient, built in 1858, when Wilder was founded by a bunch of farmers who had failed to find gold during the north Georgia gold rush. I can practically recite the facts with the same bounce in my voice my sixth-grade history teacher used during our Georgia History unit. I swear, this movie is turning into a tour of historic field-trip sites.

A creek runs up the back side of the mill, a small wooden footbridge that's still usable crossing from one side to the other. In the middle, you can see the view of the ancient, hulking waterwheel attached to the outer wall of the mill. Waterbury, two towns over, dammed up the river, which slowed the flow of water down here to a trickle. At its peak after a particularly heavy rainfall, the creek will still rise only a foot or so, not even coming close to licking the bottom of the wheel. I'm not surprised locations is using the place. With the wonder the lighting guys will work in the hazy, sunlit morning, I imagine the whole property is going to look like a fabulous fever dream.

The crew must have been working since long before sunrise, because when I arrive on set I find the lights and cameras and tents already set up for the first shot of the day. Milo and Lydia are perched on a pair of director's chairs with their names printed on the back, both surrounded by hair and makeup people who are brushing and dabbing and swiping and combing and spraying. In front of the camera, Milo's and Lydia's stand-ins are on their marks while the lights and cameras get a final adjustment.

"Red team, go!" Benny bounds up next to me at such a speed that I worry he's going to slip on the dew-damp grass and bowl me right over. He manages to stop in time, though, and raises his hands for a double high five, which turns into a low five and chest bump. "You remembered!"

"The outfit or the high five?" Tariq and Benny made it their signature move back when they were in middle school, and Naz and I, lowly elementary schoolers at the time, mimicked every move until it became *our* signature move as well.

"Okay, first of all, *this*"—he gestures up and down to his own red ensemble—"is a *uniform*. You have just earned another point for Team PA while also saving me from having to run around the studio in my underwear."

"I'm sorry, what?" Now, *there's* a picture Naz would want to see.

Benny laughs. "I told Pete, the first AD, that you were dressing up today, and he didn't believe me. He said if you didn't, I had to run around the studio in my boxers, so thank you for not leaving me hanging on this one."

"I do what I can, Benny," I reply. Which reminds me that I never sent Naz the picture she asked for. Maybe it could help soften the blow of me shutting her out this summer.

"Hey, quick selfie? You know, for the scorecard or whatever?" I pull my phone out of my pocket and glance around to make sure it won't look like we're going to take any pictures that could get us sued.

Benny throws his arm around my shoulder and pulls me in close to his side until we're practically cheek to cheek. I hold the camera out in front of us until I've got us framed up, then Benny sticks out his tongue like he's going to lick my face while also giving me bunny ears. When I snap the picture, I'm mid-laugh. It's a good one, and despite his ridiculous expression, you can see that he's still handsome. Naz is going to like it. I hope.

"And by the way, it's *Ben*!" he says, but he's laughing. He pulls me into a giant bear hug and finishes it off by giving me a noogie.

"Hey, watch the hair, *Benny*!" I say. I give him a little shove. He returns the favor with a shove on my shoulder, and before I know it we're laughing and roughhousing like a couple of fifth graders.

I hear a throat clear behind me. I turn around to see Milo is studying us, an eyebrow slightly arched, the other furrowed. "I didn't know you'd be on set today," he says. He keeps giving my outfit—I'm sorry, *uniform*—sideways glances.

I adjust my bandanna from where Benny knocked it down over my eyes and give him a final shove. He laughs and jogs away to get back to work. I give Milo a smile. "Yeah, I'm not actually working today. I just wanted to observe."

"Ah, well—" Milo starts, but Rob steps out from the tent and calls for first team before I can make it across the grass. Milo looks like he wants to say something, but he also doesn't want to keep Rob and the crew waiting, so he follows Lydia to replace their stand-ins while the hair and makeup crew wait just off camera to jump in and adjust between takes.

I find a spot to stand near video village. I want to be able to peek at the monitors so I can see what the camera sees, and possibly overhear some of the direction. They're using two cameras to shoot simultaneous close-ups of Lydia and Milo. On one of the monitors I can see Milo mouthing his lines, while on the other Lydia blots her lips on a tissue a makeup assistant has pulled out of a fanny pack.

"Don't you just love the quiet days?" Carly asks, appearing at my side.

"If only they weren't quite so early," I say. I let a yawn escape, and it travels to Carly, who stretches her arms wide and tries to suppress one of those yawn-moans. "How early did you have to get here?"

"Four," Carly replies, like that's not an ungodly hour when most respectable people should still be tucked into bed, or possibly just crawling in after a long night. Just the thought of four in the morning makes me yawn. I got up at six to be here at seven, and I barely feel human as a result.

"Hey, can I see the sides?" I ask. I know today is some kind of romantic scene, hence the scenery, but I haven't seen the actual pages for the day. I have no idea what they're shooting. Carly hands me the stapled pages, and I flip through them. There's only one scene, with only Lydia and Milo playing in it. No extras, no other cast. I skim the dialogue, not absorbing a whole lot of it, but my eyes skid to a halt over a piece of direction.

THEY KISS.

It's right there on the page, all caps, like an accusation.

Okay, I knew that Jonas, Milo's character, was the love interest of Kass, Lydia's character. And if I'd thought about it for two seconds longer, I would have realized that of course they were going to kiss. Has there ever been any piece of entertainment in the history of the world *ever* where the love interests don't kiss? Duh, of course they kiss.

But today? While I'm here and watching?

THEY KISS.

No matter how many times I read it, the words don't go away. And neither can I. If I leave now, it'll look suspicious to Milo, and possibly the rest of the crew. I'm just going to have to suck it up and watch my boyfriend kiss his superhot, super-famous ex-girlfriend.

Today is a new day indeed.

"Rolling!" Rob calls, and the rest of the crew start to echo the call like dominos, so that everyone gets the message and shuts the hell up. The boom mike may not look like much, but it can pick up all kinds of whispers and footsteps, none of which belong in the scene. Everyone on set pauses, like a scene out of *The Day the Earth Stood Still*, where they'll stay until Rob calls cut.

"And action," Rob says. Milo and Lydia launch into the dialogue, which is heavy on the flirting. I watch Milo on the monitor. He cocks his head. He gives a smile. At one point, he winks. It all looks so . . . familiar, and it's giving me a serious case of déjà vu.

I try to avoid looking at the monitor with Lydia's face on it, but every once in a while my eye drifts over to her ruby-red lips, emerald-green eyes, and the way her skin looks like ice-cold milk on-screen. The camera, as they say, loves her, and when my eyes go back to Milo's monitor, it looks like he does too.

They shoot the scene six or seven more times, both up close and with the cameras pulled back. Whatever problems Lydia was having with her lines the other day seem to have disappeared. She's amazing today playing opposite Milo. He seems to put her at ease, or maybe it's that acting out a flirty relationship with him isn't so foreign to her. I know she cheated on him, but watching them now all made up and lit the way Hollywood intended, it makes me wonder if he still has feelings for her, too.

Rob yells, "Check the gate," which Carly tells me means he's ready for them to move on to the next shot. This is the part I've been dreading. The kiss.

There's lots of discussion happening under the tent about the best place to have the kiss happen. Apparently they were originally slated to suck face on the footbridge, giving the cameras a great view of the waterwheel in the background, but now Rob doesn't like it. Milo and Lydia have migrated over to listen in on the conversation.

Rob trots over to a rock off the side of the creek and starts asking Cole, the gaffer, if he can light the space, and Allen, the director of photography, if he has everything he needs to get the shot at that angle. And before I know it, lights and cameras are in place and Milo is boosting Lydia up onto the flat top of the rock. He climbs up next to her, and Rob is telling him to lean back on his arm, but no, move it closer, yes, closer to Lydia, and telling her to lean into his chest slightly. It's like a slow-motion nightmare, only it's not going slow enough for my taste, because suddenly Rob is calling action.

I make it through exactly one take of the kiss. I watch one time as Milo cups Lydia's chin, her head tilting perfectly as he leans in, their lips meeting. I count, *one, two, three, four* . . . and the kiss is still going.

I can feel the nausea start low in my stomach, a sort of sour pit forming and rolling around with the contents of my breakfast. I'm seriously regretting those Cocoa Puffs right about now. I drop my gaze to the toes of my sneakers and try to take some deep breaths of the cool morning air, but with the sun rising higher every minute, the atmosphere suddenly feels too heavy and too hot. I really worry I might throw up.

"You okay?" Carly asks, and that's when I realize I'm still mostly staring at my shoes, taking deep yoga breaths.

I let myself look up at her and try to wipe the illness from my face. "Uh, yeah, I, uh, just left something in my car," I reply. I turn on my heel and start to head back down the dirt road. I hear Carly say that Rodney can drive me back, but that seems ridiculous. Crew parking is barely a quarter of a mile down the road, and I think if I have to wait for the crew van to show up to drive me, I'll lose my breakfast in the grass. And then I start running, know I won't be able to stop.

Seventeen

I sit in my car with the air conditioning on full blast for almost an hour. I want to leave, but I also don't want to admit defeat. And an hour feels like long enough that Milo and Lydia have thoroughly made out and finished filming the scene. At least I hope so. Regardless, hiding out in my car for more than an hour feels just as pathetic as ditching out on the day, and besides, I don't have enough gas to sit here like this and still make it home, so I shut off the car and climb out.

I don't want to go back to set just in case the world's longest make-out session is still going on, so I cross the grass to the row of trailers production brought in for the cast. Milo's is the first one, according to a sign on the door, so I knock.

"Come in," he calls.

I take a deep breath and step inside to find the nicest space that's probably ever been associated with the word "trailer." The interior has wood floors and more chrome and glass than

I've seen in *Architectural Digest*. Milo is parked on a gray suede couch paging through the script and mouthing lines. When I step into the trailer, my shoes *slap-slapp*ing on the wood floor, he looks up, his blue eyes nearly cutting me in half with their laserlike gaze.

"Hey," he says in a way that sounds like the word is taking the temperature of the room.

"Hey," I reply in a way that sends a chill into the air.

"Is everything okay?" He looks like he's waiting for me to burn the place down, but frankly I don't have the energy for that kind of rage. Between yesterday's Internet explosion and today's indignity of watching my superhot maybe-boyfriend making out with his superhot ex-girlfriend, I just feel defeated and sad.

"Yes," I say, leaning against the wall across from him. But we both know that's a lie, which just makes me feel even more pathetic. "No. I don't know."

Good one, Dee.

Milo sighs. "Look, I know that must have been hella awkward. I didn't realize you were going to be on set today, or I would have warned you."

I glance up from my feet, the whole conversation already bordering on ridiculous. "Oh? And what would you have said?"

Milo looks like I've slapped him, then he sighs. "I just, I don't know, I would have . . . It's my job?"

The silence between us more than fills the trailer. It's so big and heavy that it feels like it's trying to bust out the windows.

When it gets too much to bear, Milo drops his script onto the couch next to him and crosses the small space to me.

"Look, I know this is superweird. I get it," he says. His voice is light, like he's trying to make a joke, but it's falling flat. "Come on, every relationship has its ups and downs."

A pop of laughter bursts out of me in an explosive *ha!* "This is *hardly* a normal relationship," I say. The words escape before I have time to run them through a filter, but as soon as they're out I realize the truth of them.

"What does that mean?" Milo asks.

"None of the guys I've dated have ever sung at the Grammys. Or starred in a movie. Or had an ex-girlfriend who was named one of *People* magazine's most beautiful humans or whatever," I say. "So maybe this is normal for people in *that* situation, but it sure doesn't feel normal to me."

There's a beat of silence before he responds. "Lydia shouldn't be a factor," Milo says.

"Really? Because when I heard her telling you how she still loves you and wants you back, it sort of sounded like she *was* a factor."

Milo looks like he's been slapped. His mouth drops open like he's going to ask me what I'm talking about, but he doesn't even try. I can tell he's thinking back to that moment near the attic set, the exact moment I hear in my head daily.

"And watching you flirt with her is pretty much the worst," I say, and it feels good to let it out. I've been so afraid of sounding ridiculous complaining about Lydia that I've been pretending it wasn't an issue. But it was. It *is*.

"When did I flirt with her?"

"On camera," I say, but as the words come out, they sound feeble.

"Again, that's my *job*. Not like you flirting with that bearded PA."

My mouth drops open, my nose wrinkling in frustration. "Benny? He's an old friend."

"Yeah, looked awfully friendly to me," Milo says.

"You're being ridiculous. Benny is not the issue."

"And what is?"

There's the million-dollar question. What *is* the issue? What's my problem? What's his? Why does it feel like there's a big hurdle standing between us? I thought we were about to clear it after we kissed in the parking lot of Lowell's, but apparently my toe caught at the last second and I face-planted.

"I just feel like I don't know what's going on. I mean, you guys broke up because she cheated on you. Does that mean if she hadn't, you'd still be together?" I ask, then go to the question I really want the answer to. "Do you still have feelings for her?"

"I can't believe you have to ask me that." Milo's lips curl, making him look sort of disgusted, but I can't tell if it's the prospect of having feelings for Lydia or the fact that I would suggest it.

"I can't believe you think I wouldn't," I shoot back. "There's just so much you're not telling me about all that."

"What can I tell you that can't be dug up via Google?" Milo practically spits the words.

"That's crap and you know it," I reply.

"Excuse me?" Milo looks indignant.

"Don't give me the poor tortured celebrity story. It's all crap, as evidenced by your James Bond act at the diner. Isn't all that about keeping who you really are *off* the Internet?"

He's silent for a moment, and we both know I'm right. Sure, there's a lot of information about him out there, but how much of it is really *true*? I honestly have no idea. And faced with the fact that he's less than an open book, Milo takes a deep breath, then launches into it.

"My album sales are flat, which is appropriate since so was my last album. I want to try something different, but the label wants more of the same old crap, because even a poorly selling Milo Ritter album still sells well. And they won't leave me alone. I swear, I'm six steps away from rhyming 'love' and 'dove' just to get them off my back. And while we already talked about it, I think it bears repeating that my very famous ex-girlfriend very famously cheated on me with a very not-famous dude."

I gape at him. "Wait, is it the cheating, or the fame of the dude that bothers you?"

"Both. Or neither. I don't know, it's like I didn't know who I was without her. I'm supposed to be *the guy*, and then she goes off and hooks up with some rando."

It's not the answer I was hoping for. What I wanted to hear was something closer to *Lydia's a she-devil and we were never meant to be together to begin with. The cheating was a blessing in disguise, and I'm happy to be rid of her forever and ever, amen.* But instead, he's telling me his biggest problem with the cheating was that it was a blow to his *ego*. It's all been so thoroughly set on fire that I feel like I need to flee the scene.

"I can't tell if you're not who I thought you were, or if you're *exactly* who I thought you were," I whisper. Then I turn on my heel and go.

A door slams.

MOM

Dee? Is that you?

Another door slams.

Eighteen

It's Saturday, which means no work for the weekend, and I'm glad. I don't think I can face Milo after yesterday's fight. Did I break up with him? Did he break up with me? I shouldn't have bolted, but I was too afraid to see our conversation through to its end. But the joke's on me, because now I'm left with a mountain of ambiguity and a bundle of nerves preventing me from sorting it out.

I roll over and glance at the clock, happy to see that my week of ass-crack-of-dawn wake-ups hasn't broken me from sleeping in. I wish I could stay asleep for the entire day, but the frantic rustling from beneath my window is keeping me from drifting off again. I swear, if Mrs. Newington's cat has had another litter of kittens down there, I'm going to . . . well, have kittens as they say.

I flop out of bed and pad across the floor. I lean into the window and look down, sighing as I lean too far and my head thunks on the glass. Thankfully, it's not kittens down there. It's my mother. At least, I think that's her beneath the wide straw brim of that embarrassing hat.

I throw on a clean tank top and switch out my boxer shorts for a pair of running shorts, an item of clothing I only own thanks to my brief relationship with Trent Schneider, captain of the cross country team. Our relationship lasted exactly four days and three miles before I realized that if it continued I'd be found in a heap on the side of the road.

Outside I find my mother doing battle with the English ivy that's attempting to climb the side of the house. She's got it in her fists and is leaning back like she's about to scale our house, but it doesn't seem to want to let go. That's not stopping her from yanking while grunting like a Williams sister.

"That's how I feel," I say, which causes Mom to startle, let go of the ivy, and fly back onto her butt. The ivy winds up twisted around her ankle, and she kicks at it.

"Trouble in paradise?" she asks.

I pause. "What does that mean?"

"I think you know," she says. I can't look at her, but I can practically hear her eyebrow shooting up. When I finally glance over at her, still in a tangle of ivy but staring at me, her face soft, like she wants to hug me, I know for sure.

"How did you know?" I ask.

"I saw the picture," she says.

I couldn't be more shocked if my mother started growing ivy out of her eyeballs.

"You *saw* it?" I screech, practically tipping over the porch railing with the force of my surprise.

"I'm not clueless about the world, Deanna," she says. "I like a little celebrity gossip with my public radio."

"This is so much worse than I thought," I say. I bend over, thunking my head on the porch railing.

Mom climbs the steps and leans back on the railing next to me. She crosses her arms and sighs.

"I know he's a big star, and that's got to be really exciting," she says. "But that can suck all the oxygen out of the room."

She's describing the breathless feeling I've had so often when I'm with Milo. The feeling that someone is sitting on my chest. But it's not bad, though. It's just . . . a lot.

"I really like him, Mom."

She pulls me into a hug. "I'm glad," she says. "But I just don't want you to forget that you're a big star, too."

I take a deep breath and let it out into her shirt, smelling the sweat and dirt that are mixed there. When I lean back, she offers me a small smile.

"You want to help with the yard?" she asks.

"Do I look like I want to help with the yard?"

She laughs, then puts her arm around me as she leads me down the porch steps and into the grass. "Weeding is good for the soul, I promise," she says.

Well, my soul is in definite need of some TLC. The thing that was distracting me from the misery of my future was Milo, and now that's not even working. In fact, it's only adding to the misery. I have no art school, and possibly no boyfriend. My life *rocks*.

"So how do you tell the difference between the weeds and the actual, on-purpose plants?" I ask.

"Well, mostly it's a gut thing," she replies. She plops down in the garden bed closest to the porch, rocking back on her heels in the dirt. "Your eye just goes to the thing that shouldn't be there. I'll show you. You'll pick it up really fast."

She motions for me to scoot next to her, so I drop to my knees in the soft grass and perch at the edge of the flower bed.

"This," she says as she runs her hands over the leaves of a big green bush covered in hot-pink blossoms, "is an azalea. Everything popping up beneath it that *isn't* an azalea needs to go." She points to a patch of clover-looking greenery near the edge of the plant. I reach over, grab the leaves in my fist, and yank. They snap off, and I come away with a fistful of crumpled leaves.

My mom shakes her head. "You want to pull the whole thing out, root and all, otherwise it'll be back lickety-split." She takes her thumb and forefinger and sinks them down into the soft brown dirt right at the base of the now-decapitated clovers. She pinches and pulls, and after a second up comes a bright red root system that looks like a jumble of nerves wrapped around a tiny clump of dirt in her hand. She gives the thing a shake, dirt raining back into the small hole where the clovers once were, then tosses the weed, root and all, into a small pile in the grass behind her.

She nods as if to say *Now you*, and so I do. I scan the dirt and spot another patch of clovers. Instead of reaching for the leafy green top, this time I push my fingers down into the soil right at the base of the stem. I can feel the cool, damp dirt bury itself into the half-moons of my fingernails, but I ignore it and pull. I'm surprised by the resistance such a scrappy little plant can give, but after putting a bit of muscle into it, the roots let go and out it comes.

I pull all the clovers I can find, and then I start in on the other stuff. Random green fuzzy things and little yellow flowers that Mom says will choke anything else we plant. It feels good, yanking out all the bad stuff. Despite the sweat rolling into my eyes and the Jurassic bugs flying around my head, I find myself grunting and sighing and nearly cheering with each weed I eradicate. I let myself imagine that some of the weeds are Lydia, while others are the hot-pink screen names calling me a skank and a slut and all manner of other ugly words. I close my eyes, visualize, and yank, as if I can rid my life of them as I rid the garden of the weeds.

I work for a while, long enough that I completely lose track of time. I only stop when my pile is overflowing with evil, fuzzy greenery and my knees are whining, telling me they're done being perched upon, even on the soft grass. I yank one final root, a tough one that doesn't want to let go. I actually have to plant both feet firmly on the ground and put my back into it, and when the weed finally gives, I topple over onto my butt. I can feel the last remaining moisture in the grass that hasn't been sucked out by the hot early-morning sun soaking into my shorts. But still, I hold the weed in front of my face and give it a shake.

"Take *that,*" I say, tossing it in with the rest.

"When you're done taunting them, take them over to that yard-waste bag." Mom points toward the largest paper lunch bag I've ever seen. I glance down at my hands, which are caked with dirt, my nails now topped with little black crescents instead of the usual white.

"I was thinking of leaving them here as a warning to the others." I gesture to the next garden bed, the one we haven't started in on yet, where I swear I spot a stray dandelion cowering in fear.

"I don't think so," she says. She points at the bag again, but she's got that smile she gets when she finds me amusing, one she tries to suppress to keep me from becoming insufferable. I start gathering the weeds in my hands. I hold them away so the soil won't streak my shirt, but this just causes me to drop half of them back onto the grass. I give up and gather the whole pile in my arms and hug it to my chest. What do I care, anyway? It's not like my next stop is dinner or dancing.

Standing, I realize that my knees are none too happy about me sitting on them for the last half hour. I can practically hear them creak as I take a few tentative steps. I stop to flex a few times, feeling like the Tin Man and wishing for my own can of oil.

"Therapeutic, huh?"

"Yeah, not bad," I say. "What are you needing therapy for?"

Mom hops up from the grass and takes off her gardening gloves, dusting them off on the leg of her shorts before stuffing them into her back pocket. She takes off her hat and swipes at the sweat over her brow. "Oh, the usual," she says. "Prerelease jitters. Fear of terrible reviews. Worry that I may never write another book ever again."

I gape at her. "Holy crap, seriously?"

"Well, yeah. What did you think?"

"Uh, that by the time you're on book seventeen you're feeling pretty confident in your awesomeness?"

Mom bursts out laughing. "Some days I feel pretty awesome, sure, but others I'm a mess. And it's not like it's been a path of rose petals for all seventeen. You remember my fireman series?"

I nod, picturing the covers of the books in the trilogy, each with a glistening, shirtless fireman clutching a woman in a slinky silk dress while flames lapped around them. Definitely among the more embarrassing of her covers.

"Those were pretty well ignored, when I wasn't getting panned by reviewers. That was supposed to be a whole series, not just a trilogy, but my publisher canceled the rest."

"I had no idea," I say. Suddenly my Governor's School rejection isn't feeling like such a big deal.

Mom cocks her head at me. "Dee, are you okay?"

"It's been a rough couple of days," I tell her, glad to unburden myself, even just a little bit. "But this helped."

"Well, good," she says. "And hey, if you're going to do this again, I can pick up another garden pad for you," she calls as I make my way over to the yard-waste bag. I'm about to make a crack like the ones I usually make when chores are suggested to me, but at the last second I swallow it. Something about my mother's dedication to the erratic plant life she calls a garden lights a spark of pride. After pulling weeds for an afternoon, I think I might get it. Despite the heat and the bugs, there's something about the pulling and the yanking, seeing the progress and the dirt on your shirt. It's somehow both energizing and relaxing, and while I used to have no problem finding that through art, lately I've been in desperate need of that kind of outlet.

"That would be great, Mom," I say, and stuff the weeds and dirt down into the bag. I don't even have to turn around to know which smile she has now. I'm sure it's the big, bold, because-I'm-your-mom smile, which makes me smile the big, cheesy, yeah-I'm-your-daughter smile in return.

ANGLE ON a phone. On the screen, a photo of DEE and BENNY, smiling as Benny gives Dee bunny ears.

DEE

Was I right? AP Hotness score of 4?

NAZ

Meh, maybe a 3. What's with the outfit?

DEE

Color war

NAZ

Typical Benny insanity

Nineteen

"Are you actually going to eat that salad, or are you just art-directing it?" Carly asks as I shovel lettuce around the plate with my fork, intermittently stabbing at chicken and croutons. She reaches over and plucks one of the large parmesan shavings from my plate and pops it into her mouth.

I push the plate toward her. "It's yours if you want it," I say, and she dives into my croutons, leaving the lettuce abandoned.

My weeding-induced relaxation was short lived. By the time I returned to set on Monday, I felt as if my body's been electrified. Every time I heard footsteps or caught a glimpse of a human in my periphery, I'd jump, wondering if it was going to be Milo. But he wasn't on set at all on Monday, or Tuesday. They've been shooting only with Gillian and Paul, who have their own romantic backstory as Kass's mom and Jonas's teacher and mentor. I have no idea where Milo's been, other than not on set. I don't even know if he's still in the state, and I'm ashamed to say that I resorted to Google more than once to see if I could get any information on him. But if Milo was merely *hiding* from the press before the picture of us hit the Internet, now he's gone completely incognito. I'd call him, but he never gave me his number. And it's not like I have anywhere I can find it.

By Wednesday, I'm pretty sure that whatever I had with him is over.

At lunch I'm sitting with Carly, Benny, and the rest of the PAs, laughing along with their jokes, though I'm barely listening.

"So, what are you up to next?" Carly asks me.

I shrug. "Um, I don't know, Ruth's probably got something for me," I reply. I pick at the yeast roll still sitting on my napkin, but I leave the pieces on the table.

"No, I mean your next job. We've only got a few more days left."

I cock my head at her, like I don't understand. But as soon as she says it, I know it's true. Life on set is a weird vortex of an alternate reality, like being in a casino. There're no windows or clocks, and everyone is running around frantic at all hours of the day and night. When you're on set, you're *in it*, and it's hard to pay attention to much else. Maybe that's why it's been so easy for me to forget about art and Governor's School, or even my mom's proposed road trip to visit colleges. Okay, maybe that's a little to do with Milo, too, but they go together, don't they? So the realization that I'm about to be spit out of the vortex feels wrong, like an eviction.

Carly is staring at me, and I don't want to start crying or something embarrassing, so I laugh. "Next up for me is senior year of high school," I say, and shrug. "You know, SATs, APs, college apps." I try to sound lighthearted, but the truth is I'm dreading it. Now that I'll be starting senior year with a blank slate, I'm in desperate need of some direction. And probably a guidance counselor.

She laughs. "Ah, I always forget you're a baby."

"Thanks, I think?" I toss a crouton at her, but I miss, and it bounces off the shoulder of a burly camera guy at the next table.

After lunch, Ruth sends me on my weirdest errand yet. She hands me an armful of five oversized feathers that look like they were procured from various exotic birds. I am to take them to makeup and let them decide "which one works." Works for what, I have no idea. She says they're for a photo shoot, but doesn't elaborate.

When I arrive in makeup, I find a woman parked in the makeup chair, her hair pulled up in a bun so tight it looks like an amateur face-lift. Joanne, one of the makeup assistants, is painting the woman's face with a rainbow of primary colors. There's a red diamond over her left eye, and a blue triangle on her cheek. Joanne is working on an orange star on her neck when she notices me.

"Are those my feathers?"

"Uh, no, these are someone else's," I say. She rolls her eyes, but she's laughing. I pass them to her, and she holds each one in turn underneath the woman's face.

"I like this one," she says of a bright blue-and-green peacock feather. "What do you think?"

"It's nice?" I say. "I don't really know what it's for."

"Design is going to photograph her and use the image for a big banner that's going to hang in one of the final shots. Huge, like two stories."

I pause and really look at the makeup job and the peacock feather, along with the others now lying in a row on the table. I tilt my head a bit, then reach for a red-and-orange one that's so bright I'm sure it doesn't belong to any bird that occurs in nature. Positioned beneath the model's face, it serves as the start of the rainbow in the pattern.

"Maybe this one?" I say.

"Good eye," Joanne says, then reaches for the yellow makeup and begins working on some blending around the woman's jawline.

She hands me the other feathers to take back to props, and as I turn to leave I notice there's someone sitting in the last makeup chair all the way at the far end of the room. I almost missed him, because the bright lights of the makeup mirror cast a glare in the corner, but as soon as I see the scrollwork of fake black tattoos, I know it's him.

I don't know if he noticed me before, or if he's noticing me now for the first time, too. He shifts in the makeup chair and inhales, like he's about to say something, but the door to the makeup room opens and Ashley, another member of the crew, comes in with a brush and a tube of something.

"This should do it," she says, then squirts a dollop of what turns out to be black paint onto a small palette and sets back to work on Milo's tattoos.

He still looks like he might say something, but if it's going to turn into a repeat of the conversation we had in his trailer, I'm not interested in an audience. I quickly make my way out into the hall.

"Dee, wait."

I turn and see Milo coming out of the makeup room after me. His hands are in his pockets, his shoulders rolled in, taking a good three inches off his height.

"I'm sorry. I have nothing else to say in my defense except that I was an ass."

"Yes," I reply. I have nothing else to say either, apparently.

He shifts uncomfortably. I don't know what he was expecting me to say, but that wasn't it. "I really should have told you about Lydia. I have no intention of starting up with her again, so I just wanted to ignore the whole situation. But you're right. Hiding it made it worse."

"Yes," I say again.

"I, um . . ." He starts fiddling with a string hanging off his shirt, tugging at it and wrapping it around his index finger. The hem of the shirt pulls unnaturally with the thread.

I hear my mother's words echo in my ears. *You're a big star, too*. I take a deep breath, claiming the oxygen as my own, then reach out and swat his hand away. "Gloria's gonna kick your ass if you tear a hole in that shirt," I say.

A smile quirks at his lips, but it's faint. "Can you forgive me?"

He looks so impossibly sad and sorry and pathetic. Milo Ritter, his blue eyes clear and his soft blond hair falling over one eye, is seriously asking for my forgiveness. And he should. Because he definitely *was* an ass.

And as soon as I think it, I know I'll forgive him. I break into a smile.

"I guess I can," I say. I glance around to make sure no one's in the hall, then reach up and grab a handful of his shirt, pulling him down to me. Our lips lock, and his hand snakes around my back and pulls me closer.

When we break, he grins. "Easy on the wardrobe," he says. "Gloria's gonna kick your ass."

I smooth out the fabric of his shirt, pausing to let my hand linger on the muscles in his chest. But there's one last thing that I don't say. I'm afraid our relationship is a deer in the woods I'm trying not to spook for fear that it'll bolt back into the darkness.

Shooting wraps next week. Production will pack up and go. I'll be spit out of the vortex.

And Milo will, too.

Then what?

Twenty

RINGRINGRINGRINGRINGRINGRING

Our doorbell clangs through our house with a metallic racket that nearly causes my legs to collapse beneath me. My parents never replaced the ancient metal bell with a newer, more soothing model like I suggested. The original doorbell is literally a metal bell with a metal knocker that rattles like one of those old-timey alarm clocks, only much, *much* louder. It's enough to make your fillings jangle.

"I'll get it! I'll get it!" I shout, hurtling myself out my bedroom door and down the hall. I skid through the foyer, stopping myself by grabbing on to the heavy iron doorknob on our front door.

"If you think I'm letting you leave here with that boy without saying hello, then that time I dropped you on your head as a baby did more damage than I thought." I glance over my shoulder to see my dad leaning against the wall, arms crossed over his chest in what I imagine is meant to be an intimidating stance. Unfortunately, my dad is a five-foot-six-inch historian whose blond hair is getting awfully wispy on top and who has a difficult time keeping his round, wire-rimmed glasses on his nose.

"Please don't embarrass me," I hiss at him, trying my best to give him the puppy dog face that usually works on him. He doesn't move.

My parents have always been pretty welcoming to whoever I happen to be dating, even when he shows up wearing shiny black pleather pants and a four-foot wallet chain, yet they can't help but be suspicious of Milo. I don't blame them. They've seen his face plastered all over the glossy tabloids under headlines such as RITTER TANKS, TURNS TO DRUGS? and LYDIA AND MILO'S WILD NIGHT! after all. They're smart enough to know that most of that is crap, but they're parents. It's their job to remain skeptical.

I open the door and immediately break into a wide smile at the sight of Milo, clad in another tissue-thin V-neck, this one gray, paired with preppy khaki shorts and a pair of navy boat shoes. It's a totally bland outfit, and he's rocking it so hard I want to shimmy-shake with the beat.

"Hi! Let me grab my purse," I say, holding up a finger indicating that he should wait on the porch and maybe not come in to tangle with my dad, who is clearing his throat behind me. I see Milo glance at him, then step into the foyer.

"I'm Milo Ritter," he says, and reaches out to shake my dad's hand like he's any of the other totally normal nobody guys who've picked me up for dates (pleather pants aside). I almost laugh at how clichéd it is, watching my dad give Milo the firm, professorial handshake that he usually reserves for donors and students who don't want to turn in their term papers. It would be slightly intimidating if Milo weren't a good head taller than him. "Good to meet you, sir."

I take the moment of their innocuous greeting to grab my purse from the couch, but when I get back I find my mother has wandered out of her office in full-on draft mode. Her hair is a frizzy mess, her glasses are falling down her nose, and she's got a yellow no. 2 pencil stuck behind each ear.

"It's nice to meet you," she's saying, transferring her empty coffee mug to her left hand so she can shake Milo's. "I'm Marilyn, Dee's mother."

A flash of recognition crosses his face, and I brace for it.

"Marilyn Wilkie? As in, the romance writer?"

"That's right!" she replies. Her eyes light up, and whatever plot problem that was weighing her down drifts away. Mom always loves getting recognized, which really only happens at book conventions and signings, when she's standing in front of a full-color portrait of herself and whatever book she's promoting. I'm sure it's making her year that someone like Milo Ritter knows her name.

"You read romance novels?" I can't keep the shocked, almost mocking tone out of my voice.

"My mom," Milo says to me, then turns back to my mother. "She's a huge fan. I think she's read all your books."

"Well, isn't that just a kick! I've got a new one coming out. It's sort of a departure—" Mom says, but I cut her off with a *Please don't* look. Once she gets started talking about her work, it's nearly impossible to get her to stop, which is why I know the plot to her entire Scottish rogue series despite having never read a single word.

"I'll have to get you to sign a book for her," Milo says with a warm smile, and my heart melts like a pat of butter on hot toast. "I'll swing over to a bookstore sometime soon and then come by."

Mom gives me an *I like him* nod of approval.

"Where are you two off to tonight?" Dad asks, affecting his deep professorial voice.

"Dad, we really ought to get—"

"Vintage movie night at the Parkland Drive-In. Triple feature of the *Back to the Future* trilogy," Milo says.

Dad sighs, clutching at his chest. "It really hurts that my childhood is considered vintage," he says.

"Better than antique, dear," Mom replies.

"True," Dad says, his voice still faux-deep. "Well, on your way there, have Dee take you to Central City Park. She can show you where she—"

"*Dad!*"

Milo gives me a side eye and a slight smirk, and I know that one's going to come back to bite me at some point during the night. I'd really prefer not to tell the embarrassing story about why my parents are so hesitant to loan me the car, and why there's a magnolia tree at the north end of the park that may never be the same.

Right on cue to add to the Wilkie Family Fun Night, Rubix lopes into the foyer, his nails *click-clack*ing on the wood floor. He wanders up to Milo, does a lazy lap around his legs, and then lets all 110 pounds of yellow dog collapse in a heap on his feet. Not *at* his feet, like most respectable dogs, but *on* his feet, rendering Milo immobile. I shoot Rubix the stink eye. *Traitor.* But he just lets out a howling yawn, then settles his head down on his front paws.

"Hey, why don't you take Rubix with you?" Dad says, bending down to give the old dog a scratch behind his enormous ears. "He could use some adventure. You could walk him around the drive-in."

At the sound of his favorite word, Rubix's tail thumps heavily on the floor, but he doesn't lift his head or move from Milo's feet.

"Very funny, Dad," I say, then turn to Milo. "Rubix is afraid of loud noises. We tried to take him to the drive-in once, and he drooled an ocean in the front seat and cried through the first hour until we took him home."

"Aw, poor guy," Milo says. He bends down and gives Rubix a double-handed scratch on his big, droopy cheeks.

"Yes, yes, very sad, now we have to *go*," I say. I shoot Mom a *Help!* look.

"Yes, say good night, Ron," Mom says, winking at me and dragging my dad back down the hall.

"Call if you're going to be later than eleven!" Dad shouts before disappearing into the kitchen.

"Dad, the showing starts at nine. They'll just be starting the second movie at eleven!" I turn to Milo, who's grinning, relaxed as ever, his hands deep in his pockets. "I'm sorry. There's really no excuse for them."

"They're parents," he says. He steps to the door and gestures for me to go out ahead of him. "That's what the good ones are supposed to do."

The Parkland Drive-In is one of my favorite places in Wilder, and not just because it has the most literal name on the planet. It's been around since the fifties, though the tinny speakers on the poles have been replaced by a low-frequency radio station that you play through your car stereo. I think that's the one and only update, though. The snack bar is still a tin-roof shack where they make sliders and chili dogs and giant vats of popcorn by hand. It's only ten dollars a car for however many movies they happen to be showing that night, and with tonight's triple feature, it's a killer deal. And since the first movie doesn't start until sundown, which comes at almost nine, it won't end until almost four in the morning.

"Favorite spot?" Milo asks after he's paid the attendant.

"Middle of the middle," I reply, and he shifts the truck into drive and aims for a spot. He finds the last one in my preferred viewing location and backs the truck in, then hops out.

I follow him around to the back, where he drops the tailgate and gives me a boost into the flatbed. There's a thick blanket and a small cooler of glass-bottle Cokes.

"Sorry, I didn't bring any pillows," Milo says. He climbs in behind me, and the truck bounces and creaks under his weight. "I didn't want your dad to think I was, well . . ."

"Not a problem," I say. Milo settles into the truck, his back resting on the rear window, and I settle myself into the space between his knees, leaning back and using his chest as my pillow. He reaches into the cooler and pulls out two Cokes, twisting off the caps and handing me one.

"To summer," he says.

"To summer," I reply, and we clink the bottlenecks and take long swigs. It's been only three weeks, but already I feel like a different girl from the one who sat outside the Coffee Cup worrying about how it was going to be the worst summer of her life. It's been crazy and amazing and frustrating and interesting, but it hasn't been the worst. Not by a long shot.

Up ahead, lightning bugs dance in front of the screen until the projector roars to life. Milo reaches back and slides the window of the truck open and leans in to crank the radio so we can hear the jingle that goes along with the dancing hot dog and popcorn telling us to visit the concession stand. Then everyone starts honking as the screen goes black, calling for the movie to begin.

The screen lights up, the symphony plays the booming

theme over the Universal Pictures logo, and then there's the camera panning over the sea of ticking clocks in Doc's laboratory.

As Marty starts his race to get to school on time, I feel Milo's breath on my ear, and then it's lower, moving down to my neck. I lean back into him, breathing in and feeling myself melt. His lips start their journey from my collarbone, up my neck, on along the line of my jaw. His finger traces the path ahead of him until he's slightly tugging, and I return his kiss with the deepest of sighs.

We make it all the way to Marty McFly falling out of the tree before we give up on watching the movie entirely. We sink down into the bed of the truck, our legs tangled as our lips meet. Milo's hands go up to my hair, mine on his cheeks, and I feel like I want to devour him, he's so delicious.

But each time he kisses me, I sense the tally of remaining kisses getting smaller, like someone is tearing the pages off one of those page-a-day calendars. I don't know how many are left, but it doesn't feel like enough. And each time his lips meet mine I want to ask him how many, give me a number, please, I just need to know. Is the number bigger than I thought? Infinite, even? But I don't want him to stop kissing me *now*, so I don't ask. I'm not ready for this to be our last kiss.

Or this one.

Or this one.

It seems greedy, but it really doesn't feel like there will ever be enough. Of this. Of him. Of time. How can there ever be enough?

And so the first movie ends and the second one begins, and my lips ache from kissing him. I'm nestled deep into the nook of his shoulder, one leg thrown over him. It's only midnight, but I'm exhausted from the day and the night, and exhausted from wondering. But still, I don't ask.

Twenty-one

The next morning, I walk into the kitchen to find Mom sitting at the table in the breakfast nook, a spiral notebook flipped open to a fresh blank page. It's a sure sign that her book release is imminent, and she's trying to distract herself from the hoopla by diving headfirst into a new project. Her pen is poised over the top line, but her gaze is out the big picture window into the backyard, where Rubix is working on a hole right in the middle of the yard. She taps her pen on the blank page as she stares out the window, the motion leaving a constellation of ink marks on the otherwise blank page. As I watch her, I'm struck by how much I see myself in her, and not just the crazy hair and the freckles.

Outside, Rubix lets out a bark, then drops face-first into the dirt and begins to roll around like he's got ants in his pants.

"That damn dog," Mom mutters, but I notice a small smile.

"Hey, he learned it from watching you," I reply. Having

finished with the front yard (which, I have to admit, looks pretty impressive), she's started in on the backyard. Until recently it's just been a big, fenced-in area of patchy grass (more dirt than anything else) that serves as Rubix's play yard and doggie potty. When leaves would cover the ground each fall, Mom would simply tell us we were practicing "organic gardening" and letting everything compost. Dad would mutter something about how those words don't exactly mean what she thinks they mean, but no one ever cared enough to correct her (or dig for the ancient rake in the back of the garage). But now, the existing grass patches have been mowed to a uniform height, and straw covers all the blank spots where Mom laid grass seed the other day. And as of yesterday, there are approximately ten giant holes that Mom dug along the fence line that are going to get filled with some kind of flowering bush she's waiting on the local nursery to deliver.

"You're looking happier this morning," she says.

I pour myself a glass of orange juice and down it in two big gulps, then go for the refill. "Happier than?" I ask.

"I don't know, than when the summer began?" When I don't say anything, she tries again. "I'm guessing you had fun last night?" There's a tone in her voice that tells me she's asking more than she's asking, but I'm not ready to give it up yet. This one I'll keep for me a little longer.

"Yeah, I had a good time," I reply, trying to keep my tone light while my smile stays coy.

"I'm glad to hear that," she says, a *dot dot dot* clearly implied. When I don't fill in details, she gives up and gets to the point. "To be honest, I sort of can't believe I agreed to let you stay out that late with a boy I barely know. You were just so unhappy about the whole honors program thing, I was primed to agree to anything that might make you smile."

Rubix wanders in through the open back door and plops down at our feet, waiting for someone to offer him a biscuit or a bite of whatever's on the table.

"Does that mean I can get my nose pierced?"

"Not a chance," she says, her tone more than serious. Damn, I knew I should have kept that one in my back pocket a little longer. "Speaking of smiles, you seem to be sporting a fairly large one today. Anything I should know about?"

"Just a nice night," I say.

Mom pauses, looks like she's considering something, and then sighs. "Were you safe?"

I recoil. "God, Mom! Gross!"

She holds her hands up in mock surrender. "You know the rules. I give you your freedom, you give me your honesty."

"Well, that's *honestly* awkward, and also not even up for discussion. We've barely been going out for a minute," I tell her. "If you must know, we just kissed."

Mom can't hide her sigh of relief, even though she practically pulls a muscle trying to turn it into a regular old exhale. "I know the party line is that I'll support you in whatever choices you make for yourself, but I'm not going to lie, I'm really glad to hear that."

"Good. Can we be done with this conversation now?"

"Of course," she says, seemingly as happy to move on as I am. "New topic?"

"Sounds good to me."

Mom takes a deep breath, the kind that comes before some seriously huge parental news, and I can't help it. My mind goes to the absolute worst scenario. Are they getting divorced? That would be pretty much the most shocking thing that's ever happened to me in my life, and that includes the fact that I'm dating Milo Ritter.

She lets out the breath long and slow, then places a book on the table. The cover is all black, with a pale woman's hand holding what appears to be some kind of whip. *A Most Dangerous Game*, the cover screams in bloodred letters. The words "lust" and "whimper" leap off a blurb from the front cover, but that's not what catches my eye. I blink, but the letters don't rearrange. No matter how long I stare, the name at the bottom still says "Marilyn Wilkie."

I pick the book up off the table and turn it over in my hands. "A once-in-a-lifetime night of lust turns into a once-in-a-lifetime love . . ." reads the tag line in loopy red script. The blurb below goes on to talk about someone named Natalie and her experience with someone named Randolph, and I have to stop reading because the words are starting to blur and my stomach is starting to turn. Because this is not my mother's usual romance novel. This is not duchesses and farm boys and ripped bodices and quivering members. This is . . . well, my mother has leveled up on her romance game, apparently. Or down, depending on your perspective.

I drop the book like it's going to burn me.

"*This* is your new book?" I say when I can't take the silence anymore. I can't believe this is going to be in stores, where people I *know* can read it. "How could you not have warned me about this?"

Mom sighs. "You were so miserable; I didn't want to add to it. And then you got so busy on the movie that I guess I let it get away from me," she says. "Plus, telling your teenage daughter that you write erotica? It's, well, a little *unseemly*."

"Well, *yeah*! Ya think?" I say, my voice rising to a pitch that makes Rubix raise his head from his paws and cock his ears at us. "I can't believe you wrote this." The book is sitting on the table between us like a bikini-clad elephant.

"Are you embarrassed?" she asks.

I pause, thinking about it. I mean, I guess, knowing my *mother* was the one writing those things. It's like walking in on your parents fooling around. I know they do that stuff, and that's fine, but I do *not* need to see it.

Or read about it.

I find myself stuttering and sputtering, fighting away images that the cover and the jacket copy conjure up in my head. "I just . . . I mean . . . not really, but . . . why?"

She shrugs. "I don't know, I wanted to try something new?

Get out of my comfort zone?" She takes a sip of her tea and sits back in her chair, rolling her neck. "Being creative as a job can be exhausting. The only way to keep it fresh, to not let it drain you, is to change it up. Rock the boat."

"Well, you certainly did that," I say, and I can't help it, I laugh. Because this situation is ridiculous. Insane. It's like your mom giving you "the talk" on acid. I wonder if anyone has ever had to discuss her mother's erotica with her. But the longer I laugh, the more her words sink in. About staying fresh and rocking the boat. About how draining creativity can be, and it occurs to me that that's a little bit of what I've been going through. I've been blaming my artistic paralysis on my rejection from Governor's School, but the truth is I was having a hard time before that. I was grinding away at the same old stuff, and I was *bored.* And what finally snapped me out of it was trying a different outlet for my creativity. Working on the movie, thinking about art in a more physical way, has really gotten me excited again. And while I'm not bolting for my sketchbook, I have found myself looking at the world around me and picturing the way it would look through the lens of a camera. I've imagined props I'd move or alter to make the scenes around me more dynamic. And the excitement I get from that feels remarkably similar to what I used to feel when propped up with my sketchbook on my knee.

"Is there anything I can do?" Mom asks.

I think for a moment, since yanking the book from stores

isn't an option. Besides, if it's as popular as the other dirty books I've seen on the shelves, then this thing could more than pay for my college education.

"Just promise me I won't ever have to go to a reading," I say.

She laughs. "Deal."

Twenty-two

"Can I get a little more light over here?"

A woman in a tool belt with heavy gloves on adjusts the angle on the oversized light in the corner of the room, until the chair Rob is pointing to is bathed in a soft glow.

It's the last day of filming. We're shooting three scenes, and when we're done we'll hear Rob call *That's a wrap!* And then everyone will pack up and go, back to LA or New York, off to work on another movie or a TV show. There will be other jobs and other cities and towns. It feels sort of like what I imagine high school graduation will feel like, when everyone's off to colleges all across the country. Only with the movie, there's no promise of summer breaks and holidays back together. I'll probably never see a lot of these people ever again.

I may never see *any* of them.

There's an excitement on set as we barrel toward the finish

line. Today the entire principal cast is on set, including Paul and Gillian, whom I've barely seen since that first day in the conference room. It's still weird to me that stars as big as them can be in a movie and actually film for only a few days.

We're in the studio today, filming in a high school classroom set that's been set up in what was probably an old conference room. The set designer ripped out the flat, oddly patterned office carpet and replaced it with that ugly linoleum you see in high schools everywhere, sort of off-white with veins of brown going through it. There's a whiteboard and a caged clock on the wall and one of those big bulky teacher's desks at the front, while the rest of the room is filled with rows of classroom desks, the kind with the little table attached to one side that's never actually big enough to hold your notebook, your pen, *and* your arm.

Gillian and Lydia are sitting in two of the student desks while hair and makeup attends to them. Paul is perched on top of the teacher's desk in front of them, checking his teeth in a compact mirror for bits of his breakfast. The scene today is one where Kass and her mother are meeting with Mr. Greenfield, Jonas's mentor and Gillian's character's old flame, to talk about how Kass is bombing her classes, which her mother blames on her relationship with Jonas.

Ruth has sent me into the room with a box of props for the scene. Just general classroom-type stuff: erasers, a pen cup, a stack of books with generic spines meant to look like big classic tomes. I busy myself placing them around the room, checking every once in a while to make sure they're all in frame and not cluttering the shot. Ruth will be in to check my work and adjust things, but I want to get it right the first time.

I'm rearranging the stack of books on the desk so the colors of the spines will complement one another when Rob appears at my side.

"Dee, right?" he asks.

My heart starts to pound, and I instantly wonder what I've done wrong. I do a quick scan of the props to make sure there aren't any obvious brand labels or something showing, but I don't see anything. "Uh, yeah. Yes. That's me," I sputter.

Rob nods. "I just wanted to tell you that you've done a great job here. You seem to have a real eye for set design. Ruth's mentioned your work is good, and from working with her you probably know she's not overly effusive with praise," he says. He tilts his cap up on his head and swipes at his forehead. "And I know asking you to do those paintings was really out of left field, but they turned out great. I really think you could have a future in set design. Or studio art."

The whole time he's talking, his face remains pretty stern, like he's still really considering the words he's saying, and it's probably good. Because if he were smiling at me right now or showing even the tiniest bit of enthusiasm, I'd probably scream or cry or launch into a serious giggle fit. Partly because it's such a supremely awesome compliment, and partly because it feels so much bigger than I imagine getting accepted to Governor's School would have. I've wandered so far off the path I had imagined for my summer, and yet I wound up in almost the same—maybe even better—final destination.

"Oh, wow, thank you," I reply. For some reason I'm whispering, like we're in a church or a museum. I think it's because I know that right now I have only two volume settings, quiet and *holy wow, greatest day of my life!*

Rob reaches up and adjusts his Yankees cap. "Listen, if you decide you want to pursue this, I'm more than happy to be a reference for you."

Yup. Definitely better than Governor's School.

"Thank you," I say, my voice leaping to the upper registers. Rob winces and nods at me, and I decide to shut my mouth before I annoy him enough that he rescinds the offer.

"Okay, people, let's get going. Rehearsal?" he says. Everyone takes their places, Gillian, Lydia, and Paul on their marks, camera and lighting crew behind their equipment. Rob adjusts his headphones so he can hear the dialogue from the hall, where he'll be watching on the monitor.

"Rolling!" Rob calls, and the echoes of *rolling rolling!* bounce off the linoleum. "Action!"

The scene begins, with Paul talking in this gentle teacher voice, and Gillian answering back in a snappy, angry tone. Lydia is slumped down in her seat. After a few beats of silence, Rob calls cut.

"Lydia, your line," he says, and she jumps slightly in the desk chair.

"Oh, uh, right," she says. Kathleen hustles in with the

binder to show it to Lydia, who looks annoyed and embarrassed.

"We good?" Rob asks. Lydia nods, and Kathleen disappears back into the hall. "Okay, from the top. Action."

The scene begins again. Paul, then Gillian.

The silence.

"Lydia!" Rob snaps, and she starts her line, but it's too late. "Still rolling, from the top."

And the scene begins again. This time Lydia says her line, only she stutters over a few words. I can hear the sigh from my perch in the back corner of the room behind the camera. And so it goes, with Lydia flubbing her line or forgetting her line for the next four takes. At one point Gillian leans over to offer her a squeeze on her shoulder, a comforting gesture, but Lydia leans away from it. Her face is a mask of anger and irritation, but it's *nothing* compared to Rob.

"Okay, cut!" Rob stomps into the room. He marches over to Lydia, his hands on the desk as he leans down toward her ear. But even though his voice is hushed, the room is completely silent, and also small. Everyone can hear his every word when he tells Lydia, "I don't know if it's jitters or exhaustion or what, but take five, get yourself some coffee, and get your shit together. Got it?"

Lydia nods, then rises and bolts from the room. Rob turns to the rest of us. "Take five. Don't go far."

A few of the crew members take the mini break as an opportunity for a smoke, and hustle out the door and down the hall.

I figure this is as good a time as any for a bathroom break, since the pipes run over the ceiling of the classroom set and we've been given strict instructions not to flush during shooting.

I make my way down the hall to the bathroom. I push open the door and start to scurry into the stall when a flash of red catches my eye. It's Lydia. She's sitting on the counter right next to the sink, her knees pulled up to her chin. She's either doing some deep cleansing breaths or hyperventilating. I grimace and glance at the door, wondering if I can creep out. Maybe she hasn't noticed me.

"I just keep screwing everything up," Lydia groans into her hands.

Nope, no time to leave. She's noticed me, all right. And apparently she wants to talk. *Awesome.*

But I don't want to talk to her. I'm in a good place right now. Ruth thinks I'm good at my job and Rob just offered me a reference. And though I still don't know what happens after we wrap, for now, things are good with Milo. I don't need any more of her wry threats or sarcastic one-liners. And while I'm not one to kick a girl while she's down, I really don't feel like playing her game right now.

"Are you seriously expecting me to have sympathy for you right now?" I ask.

Lydia's head shoots up, her eyebrows rising nearly into her hairline. She did not see that coming, that's for sure. "I'm not expecting anything, but now I'm wondering what the hell *your* problem is."

I cross my arms, totally forgetting that five minutes ago I had to pee. "Uh, maybe that you've been trying to sabotage my relationship with Milo since you showed up here."

Lydia looks at me like my hair is on fire. "I absolutely have not."

"You threatened me!"

"What are you talking about?" Now she's looking at me like I should be checked into the nearest mental hospital at the earliest convenience.

I stand up, throw a hand on one hip, and kick out the other, tossing my hair back as if it were cascading waves of crimson mermaid locks. "*'The cameras are brutal. You'll never last.'*" Add a foot and a half to my height, and it's a damn good Lydia Kane impression.

She rolls her eyes. "I wasn't threatening you. I was warning you, so you wouldn't go through what I went through. The paparazzi absolutely destroyed my relationship with Milo," she says, as if it's the most obvious thing in the world, when it absolutely is *not*.

"No, I think making out with that director is what destroyed your relationship with Milo," I shoot back.

She pauses, then nods. "Okay, fair enough. But look, I still care about Milo—"

I open my mouth to tell her that's *exactly* what I'm talking about, but she holds up a finger to stop me.

"—and I want him to be happy," she finishes. "And he seems really happy with you. But if you aren't going to be able to deal with the whole press aspect, you need to get out now before you break his heart." She sighs. "Like I did."

I couldn't be more shocked than if Lydia had stacked all the fruit from craft services on top of her head and danced a cancan through the studio.

"And I know I sound all Ghost of Christmas Past or whatever, but I don't have any regrets. I mean, other than being a total bitch to Milo with that whole cheating thing. But the truth is we needed to end it. I just took the coward's way out and blew us up." When she notices I still look skeptical, she adds, "Besides, I'm seeing someone new anyway."

The old gossipmonger in me is dying to ask her who, but even though we've made out with the same guy and we're having a serious heart-to-heart right now, I still don't think I know her like that. Besides, I now know what it's like to have strangers pry into your relationship. It's not cool. When she doesn't offer up a name, I figure it's not my place to ask.

"You're nothing like I thought you'd be," I say instead. "Or what I thought you were after I actually met you, for that matter."

She laughs, then leans into the mirror, dabbing at her eyes with a paper towel. "What can I say? I contain multitudes," she replies, her tone wry. "So I take it you're going to give it a go with Milo?"

"I think so," I say, hoping I sound sure and wishing I felt it.

"Good," she says. "I think you'll be good for him. He never really did fit in with all the Hollywood bullshit anyway."

I've never been so happy to be a Hollywood outsider in my life.

The rest of the day is pretty tame. Lydia gets her line on the first take back from the break, and every time after that for all the close-ups and various shots. Then Rob calls, "Check the gate," and we move on.

The last scene we're filming is actually from the middle of the film, where Kass is watching Jonas paint in his bedroom when she gets the call that her father has died. Lydia is fantastic, a fact I can admit now that I know she's not trying to steal my boyfriend or ruin my life. When her character gets the news her face goes completely blank, then slowly starts to chip and crumble until she's a wailing pile of tears. It's incredible to watch her do take after take, each time managing to go from composed to a wreck with big, fat tears rolling down her porcelain cheeks. She's good. Really good.

And when Milo steps forward and gathers her in his arms each take, his face buried in her hair as Jonas tries to comfort Kass, I don't feel a dump truck of jealousy running me over. Not even a bit. Because I don't see Lydia and Milo, I see Kass and Jonas. It's breathtaking.

After the final take, Rob steps out from behind the monitors and shoves the roll of papers that I've come to know as his trademark into his back pocket. He removes his Yankees cap, runs his hands through his salt-and-pepper hair, and then replaces it with both hands, a big grin on his face.

"Well, people, that's a wrap!" he calls, and the crew let out a thundering of applause along with a few whoops and *woo-hoos*. I'm midclap myself when someone comes up behind me and covers my eyes.

"Guess who?" Milo asks.

I spin around. "You know, that only works when I'm not intimately acquainted with the sound of your voice," I reply with a grin.

"Oh? 'Intimately,' you say?" he says, and I instantly blush.

"You know what I mean," I say. I glance around at the crew, who're starting to break down the camera equipment and the lighting rigs. My excitement over the final shot melts away. It's over. It's really over.

My face must give me away, because Milo ducks slightly to look into my eyes. "Are you okay?"

"Uh, yeah," I tell him, though I'm mortified that I let a tiny sniffle escape. We still haven't talked about what's happening next, but whatever it is it's coming soon. I heard Lydia confirming her flight out of Atlanta. A red-eye. Tonight, after the wrap party.

Milo is unconvinced. I've proven once again that I'm no actress. But he decides to overlook my reaction, which I'm not sure I appreciate. "So I was thinking I could pick you up for the wrap party?"

"Yeah, okay," I reply, realizing this was yet another missed opportunity to figure out what happens, well, tomorrow. "Walk me out?"

Milo throws an arm around me and pulls me in close to his side. I nestle my head up into the little nook he makes for me and fall into step with him. Even though his legs are infinitely longer than mine, we fall into a comfortable stride. We make our way through the warehouse, stepping over fat bundles of cords and dodging crew members hauling equipment back into the storage lockers.

"Oh, wait, I have to say goodbye to Ruth," I say. "Mind if we make a pit stop?"

We make a quick turn and double back through the warehouse and down the hall into the prop closet. I don't see Ruth at her work table, but I hear some rustling coming from behind one of the shelves, so I make my way back. I start to call for her, but as soon as I turn down the last aisle of shelving, I'm stopped in my tracks. Leaning up against a rack of dishware is Lydia, and she's got herself draped all over a bearded guy in cargo shorts and an orange T-shirt, with socks and bandanna to match.

"Benny?" I yelp, then cover my mouth with both hands. Lydia's head snaps to me, her hair flying in a silky red sheet. Benny hops a little like he's been zapped by a jolt of electricity, then shoves both his hands into his pockets, his eyes on his shoes. "Wait, the guy you're seeing is . . . Holy crap! *Benny?*"

"It's Ben," he says, hunching his shoulders up to his ears and shuffling his feet.

"Is everything—" Milo says, skidding around the corner and smacking into my back as soon as he sees what I'm seeing. Even though they're no longer attached at the lip, it takes only one look at the pair of guilty faces for Milo to figure out what was just happening. "Wait, Lydia?"

The whole scene is ridiculous, and I can't help myself. I start to laugh—low giggles that I'm able to suppress at first, but soon they start to burst through my lips, objecting to the silence. Before long, I'm emitting borderline-hysterical laughter, the kind that makes me feel like I might just pee my pants, and I have to bend over, hands on knees, to try to contain myself. I actually have to squat because I'm so afraid the force of my laughter is going to send me toppling to the floor anyway.

"Um, Dee?" I glance up at Milo, who is looking at me like I've just gone completely bonkers. And honestly, I sort of feel like I have. "Are you okay?"

"I—" I try to tell him I'm fine, but I can't even get the words out between giggles.

"Is she okay?" Lydia asks, which somehow just sends me further into hysterical giggles.

"Seriously, Dee?" Milo squats next to me with all the patience of an orderly at a mental hospital.

I take some big gulps of air and try to let them out slowly, and I start to feel myself calming down—though a few stray giggles still sneak in. My cheeks are aching, more from trying to suppress the laughter than the actual hysterics. But I'm starting to get ahold of myself.

"I'm sorry," I gasp. "It's just that, this is all so insane, right? I mean, I'm with you"—I point at Milo—"and Lydia Kane is making out with *Benny Orazi*!" I point at Benny, who is still blushing so hard I'm surprised his cheeks haven't caught fire. "I mean, we used to play freeze tag in the Parads' backyard, and now look at us!"

Milo, Lydia, and Benny are all crowded around me now, looking at me like I've grown a second head. And then it starts. Milo cracks first, laughter sputtering out from between his pursed lips. Lydia goes next, a melodic and somewhat maniacal laugh coming from deep in her throat. And finally, red-faced Benny, who lets out the sort of geeky horse laugh that I remember from when I was twelve.

"You guys didn't get into the helium tank, did you?"

We all wheel around to find Ruth standing at the end of the aisle, arms crossed and looking like we've completely lost our minds.

Twenty-three

"Where are we going?" I ask.

I'm in Milo's truck, turning onto the highway out of town. The wrap party is at a little Italian place downtown that Rob and the rest of production has rented out for the night. It's known for its checkered tablecloths, cheesy garlic bread, and meatballs the size of your fist, so it's hard to imagine it full of Hollywood people. But we're not headed downtown.

"I figured we'd take a little drive," he says, but there's a glint in his eye that tells me he's got something in mind. With the way he keeps his eyes on the road, it's clear he's definitely not going to tell me what it is.

Milo rolls down the windows, and I sink back into my seat, my feet up on the dash, and let the warm night air blow through my hair. Tonight I'm going to do it. I'm going to ask him what happens next. I have to. It's my last chance. It's like my mother always says: *Nothing like a deadline to kick your butt into gear, right?*

I spend the drive practicing what I want to say. Or, actually, trying to figure it out. When the truck turns onto a dirt road, I still don't know. But it doesn't matter, because I suddenly realize where we are. The trees line up in neat rows in either direction, tiny dots of light from fireflies dancing around their trunks. Then the canopy of live oaks appears, and then we're pulling up in front of Westfell Grove.

The sun is starting to set, and those first fireflies are dancing around the trees in the early dusk. There was a brief storm about an hour ago, so everything smells earthy and damp. I lean my head out the window to take in a deep breath of the summer evening.

Milo puts the truck in park and climbs out, then hurries around to my side to open my door for me, since I'm too busy staring at the house to open it myself. I've never been here at night before. There's a full moon tonight, bright as a streetlight. It's sending the shadows of trees pulling along the front of the house in long, lazy angles. But something looks different. Out of place. I can't quite put my finger on it.

Milo takes my hand, the familiar calluses on his fingertips brushing along my skin. I hop down from the passenger seat, my feet landing squarely in damp dirt driveway.

"What are we doing here?"

Milo looks at the house, then back at me, practically knocking me back with the depth of his gaze. He bites his lip, then takes a deep breath. "I wanted to show you my new place."

My head snaps toward him so fast that my hair whips around and sticks to my glossed lips, which are parted in shock. I sweep it away, my hand lingering on my cheek as I try to compute what he's just said. *His new . . . Does he mean . . . ?*

I look back at the house, and I suddenly realize what looked different. It's so obvious I can't believe I missed it. The ancient plywood that covered the windows on the first floor is gone. Now you can see the rows of floor-to-ceiling french windows, all flanked by tall black shutters, that run along the front of the house. And they're new. Clean. Freshly installed. They sparkle in the moonlight. It takes my breath away.

"How?" is all I can manage, as I keep looking from Milo to the house and back again.

Milo starts toward the porch, still holding my hand, so I shuffle along behind him. We climb up on the steps, still crooked and sinking.

"I called the owner and asked him what he wanted for it. Then I offered him a little bit more to make the deal happen quickly," he says, and the glint in his eye from earlier is now a full-on light show. He's practically glowing, between his eyes and his smile and the light from the moon. He shoves his hands deep into his pockets and rocks back on his heels. "You're looking at the new owner of Westfell Grove."

"Oh my God," I whisper. There are sparklers in my chest

crackling and popping, burning a growing heat that's rising through my body up to my brain.

Milo's smile falters. "Are you good surprised? Or creeped-out surprised?"

"Good surprised!" I practically shriek the words, the full meaning of what he's done washing over me. The house is his. He has a place here. A place with me. "Definitely good."

His smile widens until it practically glows brighter than the fireflies.

"I'm just completely shocked. I was planning on asking you tonight when you were leaving, but I guess not?"

Even though this is all but an answer, I still need him to confirm it. I need him to say it. I look into his eyes, and when he shakes his head, I swear my heart turns a cartwheel. I fling myself at him, wrapping my arms around his neck and practically tackling him with such force that he lets out an *oof* of breath. The porch railing creaks behind him.

"Careful, I haven't done any work on the exterior except for the windows," he says, his voice muffled in my hair. When I finally release him, he smiles. "I'm glad you're happy. I was a little worried you were going to be freaked out. But this summer, with you, out here, I felt free. Like I didn't have to duck or hide. I realized I can't go back to LA."

It's real.

"So you're staying here," I say, waiting to hear one last time for the cheap seats in the back.

"I'm staying here," he says. "I mean, I've got to go back to

LA to pack up. I'm keeping my house for when I need to be there, and also because my accountant told me not to sell it. And obviously I need to do some serious remodeling of this place before I can move in. But yeah, I'm staying."

I can't keep my mouth from hanging open in a wide smile. It's just too good. Better than I'd hoped.

"Oh, I almost forgot." He trots back to the truck and pulls out a cardboard tube from behind the seat. He pops the top off and pulls out a roll of papers, which he unrolls on the hood of the truck. They're blueprints, the top one of the front of the house as it will look when it's restored. No more crooked shutters, no more missing panes of glass, no more sagging porch.

"So I'm going to have them restore it as close to its original beauty as possible, with a few upgrades, of course," he says.

"You mean like central air?" The sun may have set, but it still feels like a sauna out here.

He laughs. "That, and I'm going to put a studio here." He points to an outbuilding that's been added to the back of the property. "Screw my label. I'm going to do the album that I want, now and forever, even if the only person who listens to the music is you."

I shake my head, trying to wrap my brain around what's happening, but all I can focus on is the tally of kisses. It's just gotten much, much larger. As I rise up on my tiptoes to kiss him, the number doesn't subtract.

This one is a freebie.

Just One Color

ORIGINAL MOTION PICTURE SOUND TRACK

1. "Closer to You" by Brandi Carlile
2. "Starlight" by Taylor Swift
3. "Feel Like Makin' Love" by Bad Company
4. "Overkill" (acoustic) by Colin Hay
5. "Two of Us" by Aimee Mann & Michael Penn
6. "Ain't Wastin' Time No More" by the Allman Brothers Band
7. "Skinny Love" by Birdy
8. "Helpless Hands (If I Go Under)" by Hayward Williams
9. "Farewell" by Bob Dylan
10. "Love Will Come to You" by the Indigo Girls
11. "The Power of Love" by Huey Lewis and the News

Epilogue

"Nazaneen is here!" Dad calls from the hall.

Outside, I hear Naz honk twice. I take one last look in the mirror to make sure there are no visible stains on the vintage white cap-sleeve party dress I've chosen for the evening. I'm sure that's likely to change (because I'm me), but for now, I'm all good.

I grab my purse from my desk and head out into the hall, running into Dad.

"You're going to change before you go, right?" I ask.

"What's wrong with my outfit?" It's the first week in October, and classes at the college are in full swing. Dad is out of his running shorts and back in his professor uniform of khaki pants, tweedy blazers with worn elbow patches, and various threadbare button-ups. He looks fine for the classroom, but I'm hoping he'll put on something less wrinkled for tonight.

"I'll make sure he puts on something that doesn't scream

'dusty historian,'" Mom says. She's still wearing her new NYU T-shirt. We just got back from the college trip I put off all summer, visiting several schools up into New England. We visited Pratt and RISD, but now I have my heart set on NYU, where I can double-major in studio art and film. Or change my major entirely if I have another crisis of direction like the one I experienced this summer. I know now that I need to keep my options open, both for my future and for my own mental health. "Don't worry, I'm ironing my dress, too."

"We'll see you there," Dad says as I bolt for the door. Naz is honking again. She doesn't like to be kept waiting.

When I reach Naz's car, I climb into the backseat, since shotgun is occupied by Colin, the guy she met at Governor's School who she calls her "dude friend," but who is *clearly* her boyfriend. Colin lives two towns over, so he and Naz manage to see each other most weekends. I don't mind sharing her, since she forgave me for the unfortunate lies of omission I told via text over the summer. Turns out she was spending quite a lot of her summer operating her own heat-seeking missiles at one sandy-haired aerospace engineer. She and Colin are so perfect for each other that she overlooks his love of the Yankees.

"Hey, Colin," I say as I buckle my seat belt.

"What?" He jumps a little, like my presence in the car surprised him, even though Naz has been honking for five minutes now.

"Excuse him," she says, putting on her blinker as she pulls away from the curb. "He's still sort of jittery about tonight."

"Am not," Colin says, but his tone is clipped, and from my spot in the backseat I can watch him rub the back of his neck repeatedly.

"He's just a person," I say. It's the refrain I've been using since senior year began and pretty much every single person in my school, whether I'd met them before or not, tried to find a way to ask me about Milo.

"I *know*," Colin says.

"Besides, he's taken," Naz adds, and Colin blushes.

When we arrive at the familiar old dirt lane, the crumbling brick gate is gone, replaced by a shiny new iron gate with a call box. Naz pulls up and rolls down the back window so I can lean out and enter the code. The gate smoothly, silently glides open.

The property still has the same majestic quality as before, with the canopy of trees hanging low over the driveway, but it's gussied up quite a bit now. The leaves of the pecan trees are just starting to turn golden. It'll be a few weeks before the grove is blazing red. The grass has been trimmed, all the errant weeds removed. Overall it's just a better version of itself, like it's dressed up for the first day of school. Even the dirt road feels more groomed and orderly.

But it's nothing compared to the house itself. The last of the remodeling finished last week with an exterior paint job.

The peeling, moldy old siding is now a bright, spotless white. The shutters have all been repaired and coated in black, and the front door, with its newly installed stained glass, is made of oak and shiny with lacquer. Lights twinkle in nearly all the windows, making the house look alive for the first time in a very long time.

"It's still weird to me that you're dating someone who *owns a house*," Naz says.

"If only that were the weirdest thing about him," I reply. "Did you know he actually *likes* pimiento cheese?"

"Ewwww," Naz and Colin groan in unison.

There are already at least a dozen cars parking in the driveway. We let ourselves in, our shoes squeaking on the refinished floors.

"Dee! Welcome. Place looks great, huh?" Miranda, Milo's manager, is standing at the foot of the curved staircase. She barely looks up from the screen of her phone, where she's furiously typing with her thumbs, her stick-straight blowout falling down over her hands so we can't see what she's writing.

"It's amazing," I reply. I'm still getting used to Miranda and the way she's always doing six things at once. And one of those things is pretty much always "managing" our relationship. But I can't hate her. She's the one who keeps the press away from me.

Miranda finishes whatever furious message she was sending, then slides her phone into the back pocket of her skinny jeans and nods. "I was a little wary about the purchase, but I think the publicity from the design magazines is going to pay dividends."

"Also it's a really nice place to live," Naz says.

Miranda cocks her head to the side and blinks. "Oh, sure," she says. "Of course."

"Everyone's out back?" I ask. She nods, so I lead Naz and Colin through the house.

We head down the hall and cut through the kitchen, now outfitted with a collection of appliances worth of the Culinary Institute, though Milo can pretty much only make popcorn. We step through the french doors onto the back porch, which wraps around from the front of the house, and then step onto the newly laid stone path in the backyard.

The lawn is bright green and mowed in perfectly geometric rows. At the far end, a large screen has been erected. Strings of white lights crisscross the yard from the back porch to the new recording studio Milo had built. Metal buckets full of ice and sodas in glass bottles dot the yard. A buffet table is set up at one end with burgers, dogs, and all the fixin's, plus an old-fashioned popcorn machine that's giving the air a buttery tinge.

"Oh my God, it's *her*," Naz whispers through clenched teeth. Colin visibly tenses next to her. Across the yard I spot a familiar head of red hair. Lydia turns, catches sight of me, and stalks across the new grass. Quite a feat considering she's wearing four-inch heels.

"Dee! It's *so* good to see you," Lydia says. "The bar won't serve me. God, Milo's such a Boy Scout." She changes her posture to imitate the bartender, her manicured fingers hooking air quotes. "'House rules,'" she grumbles in a low Southern twang, reminding me yet again that she's a *really* good actress.

"Also the rules of the state of Georgia," Naz says.

"Actually, I think the drinking age is federal," Colin adds.

Lydia rolls her eyes, but Naz and Colin barely notice. They're too busy discussing alcohol laws by state.

Benny comes trotting over with two open Coke bottles and hands one to Lydia. I haven't seen him since production wrapped. He headed out to LA to work on some action movie starring a retired football player, which was conveniently where Lydia ended up as well, filming on some fancy cable show where they're allowed to swear. Tonight, he's wearing jeans and a plaid shirt, the sleeves rolled at the elbows.

"Nice outfit," I say.

"I was *very* glad to discover he had other clothes," Lydia says, and we all laugh.

The rest of the crowd is made up of a mix of strangers and familiar faces. It turns out I was wrong when I thought I'd never see a lot of these people again. The crew, most of whom are actually from Atlanta, are working on other productions around the state. Carly and I met for lunch when I went to tour Emory with my mom. And now a lot of them are here, brought back by the promise of an open bar and a free screening. And it's not just the locals. I spot Gillian with a box of popcorn, and Paul is setting up a pair of folding chairs for himself and his wife, another indie actress whose name I can't remember.

"Hey, isn't that that guy from that thing?" Colin asks, trying (and failing) to be inconspicuous as his eyes dart over toward Paul.

I scan the yard, but don't see the familiar blond head anywhere. "I'm gonna go find Milo," I say, then head back into the house. I make my way upstairs and down the hall to his bedroom. The door is cracked open, so I knock lightly as I peer in. He's standing in front of an antique full-length mirror, looking like he's making an attempt at a pep talk.

"Oh, thank God," he says when he spots me. He lets out a long, shaky breath.

"What's up?" I ask as soon as I notice the deep canyon of nervousness between his brows.

"I'm *freaking out,*" Milo says, each word punctuated hard.

"Why?"

"This is my first movie. What if I suck? What if people hate it as much as they hated my last album? What'll I do then?"

"Take up scuba diving?"

Milo laughs.

"Seriously, those are your friends out there. They support you no matter what," I say. "And let me be the first to tell you that you categorically *don't* suck. I watched you every day on those monitors. You were phenomenal."

Milo sighs, as if someone's let the air out of him. His

shoulders relax, and he steps toward me, his arms snaking around my waist.

"I don't know what I'd do without you," Milo says.

"Probably burn this house down, because I know you don't know how to use that monster stove down there."

Milo grins, then bends down and kisses me long and hard. I let my hands go up to his hair as I sigh into him. I wish we could stay up here all night, but there's a crowd in the backyard waiting for a screening. And that crowd includes Milo's mother and my parents, who like Milo a lot, but they're still wary of the whole my-boyfriend-owns-his-own-home situation.

I take his hand and start to lead him out of the room when something catches my eye. On the wall over his bed is a painting in a rustic wooden frame. It's midnight blue with swooshes of beige, reminiscent of sawdust floating through a darkened warehouse. Around the edges, you can still see the smudges from where the canvas was stacked and discarded before the paint had fully dried.

"That's my painting," I say, staring first at the canvas, then at Milo, who is grinning. "Where did you get it?"

"I took it from the prop room after filming," he says. "I liked it. Every time I look at it I think of that first time we talked, when I walked in on you covered in paint and in your crazy artistic zone."

"I can't believe you stole it," I say, my voice barely above a whisper, drowned out in my head by the pounding of my own heart.

“*Rescued* it,” he says, bending down to plant a soft kiss on the tip of my nose. “It’s not uncommon for people to take things from set when filming is done. Mementos, you know.”

A wide smile spreads across my face, and I have to bite my bottom lip to keep it from flattening me with joy. “So you’re a common thief!”

“Yes, well, I’m quite the bad boy,” he replies. He winks and raises an eyebrow, and I can’t help myself. I crash into him as if I’ve been shoved, meeting his chest with an *oof*, and then kiss him so hard and so long I swear the movie must be over by the time we part.

“Okay, we’re going to have to leave now, or we’re never gonna,” Milo whispers, his lips still brushing mine.

“Ugh . . . ,” I groan, but I take the hand he offers me and follow him out of the room.

Outside, more people are starting to set up lawn chairs for the screening. I spot my parents with a pair of navy canvas chairs near the back. When Dad spots us, he waves us over.

“Tremendous job with the house, Milo,” he says, sticking out a hand for one of those manly handshakes that look like they might separate your shoulder. “Really amazing. Just top-notch.”

I look over and see Milo actually blushing. “Thanks, Dr. Wilkie.”

“Call me Ron,” Dad says.

“Oh, okay,” he replies, but he doesn’t use my dad’s first name. I think he’s still a little intimidated, despite having a good six inches on Dad. Milo told me once that in all those years of dating Lydia, he never actually met her parents, making my dad the first father he's had to come home to, so to speak. It's adorable, and I know it makes my dad feel better about the whole my-teenage-daughter-is-dating-a-pop-star-turned-actor situation. "Listen, I've got all the paperwork filled out for the historical society to get the designation and the plaque for the property. I'll text you about when we can sit down to go over it?"

And with that, I think my dad loses all sense of reservation about our relationship, because he practically levitates with excitement. I swear, he grows at least an inch at the prospect of getting Westfell Grove on the National Register of Historic Places.

"Sounds good!" he sputters, raising his glass to us. I roll my eyes. My dad is such a dork, but I love him.

Up near the screen, I notice a familiar Yankees cap. Rob gives a loud whistle using two fingers, and the chattering crowd quiets. Milo and I quickly make our way to a pair of chairs right down front.

"All right, everyone. I'm very pleased to be back in Georgia for the very first screening of *Just One Color*," he says to a smattering of applause and a few *woo-hoos* (which come from my father's general direction). "Though I'm pretty thankful we're back here in October and not June."

The crowd laughs, as the out-of-towners fan themselves with whatever they have on hand. They're not conditioned to find low seventies and humid to be cool like we are. This is straight-up autumn for us.

"This is the first time anyone outside of the production team has seen the film. Our official premiere date is still a few weeks away, so if you haven't signed your confidentiality agreements, please do." This time it's the locals who laugh, but from the look on Rob's face I'm not entirely sure he's joking.

Just as the last ray of sun sets, Rob claps his hands and steps to the left of the screen. "Okay! Here now, *Just One Color.*"

The crowd applauds, and someone somewhere pulls the plug on the twinkle lights overhead. As the screen lights up silver, I lean my head onto Milo's shoulder and lace my fingers with his.

ROLL CREDITS

Acknowledgments

Thanks to my editor, Wendy Loggia, who saved me from writing bad fan fiction and dragged me kicking and screaming onto SnapChat. This book would not be this book without you. Thanks to everyone at Delacorte Press for your hard work and support, especially Krista Vitola. Thank you to my agent, Stephen Barbara. You're the very best there is, and I thank my lucky stars daily that you're on my side.

Thanks, Rachel Simon, Lenore Appelhans, and Kathryn Holmes for reading very early versions of this novel, and Vania Stoyanova and Jackson Pearce for pre-baby writing dates (someday I'll leave the house again, guys, I swear). Thanks to Amanda Blocker for making Mystic Falls so fun and for making me want to write this book. Thank you to the Little Shop of Stories, especially Diane Capriola for welcoming me into the shop and Kim Jones for making me feel like a straight-up superstar. And thank you to my author-mom friends on

Twitter, especially Sarah Dessen, Melissa Walker, and Jen Calonita, who gave much-needed advice and encouragement as I wrote a novel with a newborn.

I've been working on this book, in some form or fashion, for about three years, but it wasn't until I had a baby and a deadline three months later that things got real. So thank you to Freddie, who took lots of naps in the backseat of the car so Mommy could write this book in parking lots. I love you I love you I love you. And thank you to Adam, without whom I surely wouldn't survive.

About the Author

Lauren Morrill grew up in Maryville, Tennessee, where she was a short-term Girl Scout, a (not-so) proud member of the marching band, and a troublemaking editor for the school newspaper. She lives in Macon, Georgia, with her family, and when she's not writing, she spends a lot of hours on the track getting knocked around playing roller derby.